First Published 1985 by
IRON Press, 5 Marden Terrace
Cullercoats, North Shields
Tyne & Wear NE30 4PD
Tel: Tyneside (091) 2531901

Printed by
Tyneside Free Press Workshop
5 Charlotte Square
Newcastle upon Tyne

Typeset by Janet Hall
Book design and paste-up by Norman Davidson

The following stories were originally published
in IRON Magazine, *Joffy, Elise, Creeping About,
Chickens* and *Minimal Damage. Dark Cube* was
originally published in Raven magazine.

ISBN 0 906228 21 1, Price £3.00

supported by
NORTHERN
ARTS

SLEEPLESS NIGHTS

Stories by
DAVID ALMOND

IRON PRESS

The Stories

Elise

It was 1982. I was over thirty, and still dreamed of her.

All that summer I'd been working on a television film, a dramatisation of an 1847 mining disaster, in which a collapsed shaft had blocked off miles of underground passageway. For half a century the bodies of dozens of men and boys had been left there, until new equipment had enabled the passageways to be opened again. The bones were lifted out, and soon the darkness rang again with the noise of pickaxes, harsh laughter, controlled explosions.

It was November when her card, the sun rising over Californian surf, arrived. It bore only the scrawled message, 'No one else. Only you.', and named her hotel, gave the date she would be there.

The 25th. I sat in the dark studio, watched the final version of the film, then drank wine all afternoon, congratulated myself and my colleagues. I went out, to the sun already hanging low over the skyline, to the crowds hurrying home. Through unnecessary streets I walked slow spirals, with her high hotel at their centre....

Elise. She said she was going from the fringes to the core, from wastelands to civilisation. In 1970 a scholarship took her away from Newcastle to the psychiatric institutes of Central Europe. She promised to write to me and I knew she would not. She had already been gone from me for years. We separated at the barriers of a railway station and I soon returned to the worn-out villages of Durham, began my long task of gathering and cataloguing their past — an archivist, scratching surfaces, tugging away turf to expose the ash beneath. Held to all that even by my name, Henry, a family name, generations-long, that even corrupted to Harry seemed old, cumbersome; and she spun away by hers, Elise, an exoticism, a name with which to enter the world.

Born within weeks of each other in houses that opened onto the same narrow street, we shared the privelege of cleverness, and grew together in small warm rooms, dark streets that ended in hawthorn hedged tussocky fields, schools of stone, cast-iron railings, high windows and bare walls; always competing with each other, but grinning at each other, laughing, even before we were aware of our privilege performing it, announcing it. She was tiny, dark-eyed, her hair glistening coal. Even as an infant I dreamed her dancing, on tiptoe, hardly a connection between herself and the ground.

Continually 'doing well', showing 'great promise', we were destined, we were told, to escape our skyline of pitheaps, winding gear, furnaces.

"I don't know where you get it from," my father said, "but use it, lad. Use it."

1

My father. Like Elise's father had been before he finally submitted to the wounds of war and was lowered into an early grave, a pitman, disappearing day after day into the earth to shave the last of its old seams, shuffled from pit to closing pit, his lungs constantly tightening; who could not be convinced that the sun did not orbit a still earth, but who saw all bright futures as educated ones, who bore a fierce pride for his work and his home but who pushed me away from it all towards an imagined outside world of opportunity and light.

"You're what we've worked for," he said, "Not just in my time, but for generations. We've sweated in darkness and died for you, so you can be who you are, so you can be free of it all. Think of Elise's father — it's up to the ones like you to make his death mean something. Think of yourself, coming from your mother's dead womb. Make it mean something, Harry. Make it mean something."

Freedom, privilege, the sacrifices made by others, were the themes imposed on our youth. We were watched constantly, guided, encouraged by parents and teachers to imagine a shining future for ourselves. Elise did imagine, and she began to stretch towards that future as to a shining light, while I held back, and saw the light as nothing but a dull gleam, an illusion even, something I wished to retreat from, in order to investigate the place from which I came, and the ages of work that filled it. And even our first real exit from the villages, when we went together to the university at Newcastle, was a stage in my retreat, for I read history, began burrowing into time; and a stage in our separation, for Elise leapt into the abstract intricacies of mind and soul. She said I would find nothing but gloom. She said the mind was the body's privilege, as we were the privilege of history, and we should explore those privileges, see how far they could go.

It might have been easy to end there, had we shared only childhood, classrooms, narrow streets. But we had lain together in hedged fields, sheltered by hawthorn and gorse, with the village lights shining through stems and Consett's foundries sparkling and flashing against the stars, and we had learned there how to go so far into each other that all our oppositions were cancelled in the stillness cultivated by tenderness and touch. Those nights, that already stretched back for years, she was truly with me, and not tugging from me, but lay with her head on me, whispered of love, shared futures, care. They were our only meeting-place, my one desire. I could not, did not want to, grow free of them.

Elise tried. She pulled me in from the landscape. Many were the evenings we spent in the small flat above her mother's shop, a shop that tried to cater to every need and that kept her mother downstairs until late, when she had resisted my touch and listened to Dylan's wailing

2

against restrictions I had to struggle to comprehend. She pulled me to the city, and each morning, as we travelled across the suburbs' edge, she flew from me, spinning on a long leash of words, testing against me her theories, speculations, imaginings: those words that were so praised and rewarded by others, that made her the wild but brilliant star of her year. I did not know her there, in Newcastle, her platform, where she became a hard and distant foreign thing, dancing away from her birthplace. It became a fierce dance: she railed against the world and its constraints, marched and chanted against far-off hunger, ignorance, foreign wars. And she began to hate. Durham, she said, was a place of waste and dereliction, its people heavy and grim, unemerged from darkness. She said she could free herself of all its inhibitions, and she left it behind, rented a flat in the city. When I visited her there, it was as an intruder, a weight of lead among her new friends, their elusive words and confusing drugs.

Everywhere I was out of place. Even my father rebuked me, saw my changing as dissolution rather than growth. He chided my appearance, my grown hair and beard, my carefully disordered dress, saw it as an insult to his pride in me, accused me of a lack of the self-respect that in him was so strong. And when I mumbled that his standards, the standards of the past, had brought us only corruption, wars and injustice, and must be challenged, ignored, repudiated, he laughed bitterly.

"Challenge?" he said, "You don't challenge anything. You just squander everything, use it up. The whole lot's going to waste, because of you and your kind."

I knew nothing, understood nothing. My father's world, Elise's world — they were extremities between which I floundered, ignorant and confused. All I could hold on to were those rare nights when I stayed with her, and she at last lay with her head on me, exhausted, and told me I was the only one, the only real one, and I persuaded myself that I believed her, and that I might always be her dumb, impassive, but somehow her necessary partner, the centre of her spirals and dances, the core of her electric coil.

The persuasion was empty, the belief feigned. There was nothing, outside the uncommon unity of our sexual desires, with which to unite our lives.

Our last summer together we spent travelling, hitchhiked across Europe with a few pounds in our pockets and sleeping bags rolled across our backs, greeted hundreds of others like ourselves, all foreignness cancelled by our shared imitation of some vast ideal of freedom. On warm beaches I began to feel a loosening, and hoped that we might find there some new alternative to hedged fields, but for Elise it was far from enough. She had no respect for immobility, calm. We moved constantly from place to place, came to know nowhere except on its surfaces, saw more and moved more in one summer's vaction than we had in our whole lives, and returned with nothing but dissatisfaction in our hearts. And she detested it, the return, to this place, this ignorant Northern province — a place to leave, she said, a place from which to leap.

It was not long before she leapt. My final memories of my youth gather around the day we graduated. Photographed, her eyes stare beyond the camera, she leans forward, braced for movement, while I beside her shuffle on the grass, my eyes downcast.

Within days she was gone, stepping eagerly away from me, showing only the shine of her hair as it swung about her shoulders, the rapid swaying of her narrow hips; her mother beside me at the barrier, calling to her to write soon, and I knowing that she would not, that she had left this place, and all of us in it, behind.

I remained in Newcastle for one more year, a research student, digging into Durham's past. I rented a tiny flat in the city, lined its walls with books, maps and charts, but the villages and their landscape were my true studying-place, that I travelled to as I had once travelled from them to the university. During that year my father was forced to withdraw from his work, his lungs so weakened that within months he was unable even to climb the narrow stairs in his home, and its small ground floor became his only habitation. With the aid of walking sticks, he explored constantly his small territory, kept it neat and clean, called through the open windows to the street, hailing his old friends. Seeing him suddenly so aged, wrecked by his life, I offered to go back there and care for him, but he would have none of it. His new adversities seemed to have strengthened his stubborn independence and pride. When I did visit him, we quarrelled. He scorned my work, could see no point in it. Why should I study this, he asked, when there was a whole outside world to learn? All I did was to disturb dead men's bones. Look at Elise, he said, how well she has grasped her opportunities.

But when I went to Elise's mother's shop I was welcomed with tears of affection, and it was I who was praised, Elise who was scorned.

"My girl has disappeared," she said, "We weren't good enough for her. Why do we put so much into our children when all they want in the end is to get away from us? She's taken part of me away with her, Harry, and she won't even tell me where to. She answers nothing. She wants nothing to do with us. She's gone. It's like she's cut out my heart, and stolen it."

Elise was disappearing from me, too, but it was not like being stolen from, for beside the pain of her loss was the relief of not having to pursue

4

her, to make the constant effort of keeping her in sight. Even the memory of her began to fade, to be obscured by my work, and appeared with less frequency, until it became a distant, hidden thing, that squatted in my darkness. It hid there with the part of me that could exist only in her presence, the part of me that had grown with her, a past me that I did not want to explore as I now explored my social, historical past. I wanted to leave it there, and for that reason I decided not to travel far, for during a final holiday in Europe, alone, I found myself constantly watching for her, as if autobahns were the back streets of my villages, and the Alps reclaimed pitheaps.

My second graduation over, I began to train as an archivist to the libraries of Durham, and came to an arrangement with my father in which we shared his home, I with my accommodation in the upstairs rooms. His ceiling, my floor, was the constant reminder of the barriers between us, until he began to enter, prematurely, that strange senility which is like childhood, but childhood burdened with memory. His resistance dissipated before it, and he leaned to me as to an adult, allowed me to cook for him, dress him, while his mind wandered through a past whose clarity obscured all else. In the days before his death he maintained a spoken narrative that was like the narrative of present scenery, present events. His body tended by me, he inhabited a world of shafts and seams, the blows of chisels and the thuds of explosions. He spoke of war and of returning from war, to his few month's marriage, of lying on a white bed with my mother, the sun streaming across them from a luminous lark-filled sky, of his loss of that at my birth, his entry into the earth, becoming the scurrying dark root of a glistening future. He spoke his whole life, a chronology of small events leading to me, my disappointing life, my disappointing return to my old home.

"...Henry is back and he lives upstairs. He walks on the ceiling, waiting for me to die. The whole house will be his then, all of it, and he will live in it like me. He will become like me, nothing but me..."

It collapsed into the tired wheezing of his lungs, and his eyes staring through me to the walls. I sat by his bed waiting, watched his entry into a final silent darkness, then helped lower him into the earth, scattered a handful of it onto him, walked away from him, dead root.

With Elise gone, my father dead, the house my own, my work the work I desired, it seemed I had achieved a condition of independence, which may be all we can know of freedom. My adolescence gone, I was myself, a separate being, and I accepted that separation, began to live with it.

The villages, that had been expected to become derelict, unpopulated, as the pits closed, began to flourish. All around me young families moved

5

into the old cottages, began to knock down interior walls, brought in fashionable furniture, light. House fronts were painted, brightening the narrow streets. New estates spread onto the hillsides between villages. A new generation of children grew, who gathered in large new schools. Their eyes looked outward, towards the city, or to the new countryside, where waggonways had become signposted footpaths, stations museums, pitheaps landscaped hills where they went sunbathing and picnicking in summer.

Elise's mother prospered. Her shop was stocked with wine, exotic foods. She employed assistants, bought a car. Her unexpected freedom allowed her to travel, and she spent holidays in the sun — Spain, Majorca, the south of France. One summer she returned with a man at her side. They walked arm in arm, he saying that all of his expectations of the north had been reversed. He bought an old pit manager's house, filled its gardens with roses, flowering shrubs. Within months she had sold the shop and they were married. I sat by them at the wedding, best man, spoke to the guests of renewal, change, of how this couple stepped with such optimism into their shared future. I looked down at Elise's mother, and smiled at her, but even on that day the old pain of her daughter's disappearance haunted her eyes.

I stayed in my father's house, refused to change it. I kept the old furniture, covered painted surfaces with paint of an unchanged colour, disentangled long-planted flowers from weeds. I was offered grants with which to improve plumbing, heating, insulation, but I wanted none of them, wanted not to be part of the thrust into what I saw as a counterfeit, unrooted existence. I began writing books, histories of individual pits, that brought me invitations to lecture throughout the country, to participate in radio and television programmes. Acknowledged as an expert in the flourishing field of industrial history and archaeology, I wondered whether at last my father might have understood me, and have been proud of me.

There were women in my life, of course. A succession of them — librarians, teachers, researchers, journalists. But we made only slight, superficial attachments. Several times I was accused of a coldness, of an inability to give myself, but it was an inability shared by us all. Our encounters were a plundering of each other, an effort to satisfy desire, nothing more. At times I wanted to discard, or to ignore, my need of such encounters, but desire presses hard, no matter how meagre its final satisfaction might be, so I had to accept its pestering and its impotence. Those nights years ago with Elise, our achieved meeting of our bodies and minds, beyond intelligence, ambition or privilege, I saw now as an illusion, or as something achievable only within the circumstances of innocence and youth, circumstances which soon disintegrate. And I looked forward to the time when that disintegration might be further advanced, when desire stilled of its own accord, when I might be able to make the choice I assumed had been made by Elise's mother — for companionship, an unphysical sharing of money, time and adult circumstance, a shared understanding of inevitable ageing, inevitable loss.

Already, then, I felt old. I looked forward to my continued hewing of the past, to my decay, to immobility. Beyond that, I assumed, senility waited. There seemed nothing more....

She was asleep. On the highest floor of the hotel I found her door ajar. The usual hotel room — narrow bed, dressing table with furred stool, thin mirror-fronted wardrobe with her unopened suitcases beside it, and the wide armchair in which her small curled body was contained; below the harsh light of a spotlamp, her face turned from me, in her hair grey already beginning to overtake the black. For minutes I stood over her, reluctant to wake her.

"Elise," I whispered. I wanted to leave, to retreat from it all. But again I said it, more loudly.

"Elise."

It was the same Elise, her eyes even within their sleep-swollen rims glistening as always when she smiled. She stood, and hugged me in a gesture of welcome so sudden I could not respond to it. I found my lips pressed to the angle of her cheek and throat, my arms hanging stiffly at my sides.

"Oh, Harry," she said, touching me, my hands, my shoulders, as if to reassure herself that I was real, "I thought you mustn't be coming. I thought you must have moved, and hadn't heard from me. Harry, let me look at you."

I was grinning stupidly. Before her enthusiasm I felt dull, almost surly. I was aware of the sour taste of alcohol on my breath. I couldn't find the words with which to respond to her welcome, as if there were some constriction on my throat.

"You look tired," I said.

"It's the travelling. I don't know if I should be awake or asleep." There was an American drawl in her voice, and an excitement she seemed to demand I should share. She was on her way to Geneva, from the States.

"I found I could stop over here. I thought, why not? Come and sit by me. How good you look, Harry. Are you really still in the same place?"

She placed the stool before her chair, and we sat facing each other, our knees touching, her hands gripping mine.

"My father's house? Yes. He's dead now."

7

She wanted me to tell her about myself, but I found I was reluctant to mention anything in which she might see merit. I feared that beneath my sullenness years of bitterness and spite waited. I told her I worked in the archives, and she nodded eagerly, said how satisfying that must be. Only when I told her of her mother's marriage did her smile fall. But then she shrugged.

"Mother. Do you want me to feel terrible about that? I don't know, it's been a long time. I'm past it now."

"She'd love to see you."

"You didn't tell her?"

"About this, no. I haven't been able to look at her."

"Good. It's best. It would solve nothing now. You know, after I'd gone, it took me months to get away from it all. I kept looking out for you. I expected you on every street corner. I thought, I can't get away with this."

"You were gone for good. I knew that. We had our own lives to live."

"Yes, of course." Her voice rose, as if she were angry. "You, yes. But her?"

"What do you know about it? She thought you'd rejected her. All she wants is for you to go back."

"She could have found me. It wouldn't have been too difficult."

"You're blaming her?"

"No."

"Well, then."

Perhaps we both realised that we had entered too early an area that contained too many traps for us. We became silent, until she relaxed again, and laughed.

"Imagine. If I came all this way and all we did was quarrel."

"Why did you come?"

"I'm not sure. I suppose because I could, that's all."

I recognised her grin. It tried to stare me out, to provoke me. It waited for my grinned response.

"When I got here I wished I hadn't. I thought everybody was staring. All the way in the taxi I kept right down in the seat." Her voice suddenly filled with the lovely remnants of her childhood accent. "And I haven't dared go out."

I wanted to tell her she was childish, too selfish to face up to the harm she had caused. I said,

"You must be hungry, then."

We ordered a meal that we ate from plastic trays balanced on our knees. We had Champagne — in celebration, she said. She said she was

8

reminded of the evenings above her mother's shop, when we shared suppers of sandwiches and lager, but that we needed music. She turned on the radio above her bed, but found only orchestrations of sad Beatles tunes. She sniggered, and turned back to me, blinking away tears, on her face a wide sad smile I'd never seen before. And I smiled too, for here beside me was Elise, and somewhere here was a joke that both of us could share.

I began to talk of myself more easily. I discovered a pride in my accomplishments, and also the anger and regret that accompanied it. I told her of the new film, that was to be shown by the whole network, and said that whatever success I had was the result not of ambition, but of a desire to present the realities of the past, to set them in harsh contrast to our bland modernity.

"You wouldn't recognise Durham," I said, "The things they've done. Even Consett's finished now. Once the men who worked there are dead or gone, it'll be like the rest — a sleeping place, a place for picnics and country walks. It'll be an exhibit. A pound to see a cut-out heart."

"I know," she said, "I heard about it."

"Of course. News travels."

"It wouldn't have mattered, I admit that. But I connected it with you. I knew it would still matter to you, and that you'd still be here. I couldn't imagine you anywhere else."

"No. It was always enough."

We had no polite, unaffecting pleasantries to share. Each word was rooted in the tangles of our past, in the old separateness of our desires. Each word tugged at my pain, but Elise seemed, as always, to be protected from them, by her carelessness, her indifference. When she began to speak of herself, it was without apology or regret, with an unembarrassed eagerness. She had a story to recount, that she believed would interest me. She could not conceive that it might harm me. But Elise's world could never exist in description, in uninvolving narrative.

"And you?" I said, "What happened?"

"Oh, I was in Switzerland that year. Then anywhere. Paris, Munich, New York. Even London for a while, six or seven years ago. But I seem to be settling now. I've even got my own house."

And she brought out a photograph. Houses stretching for miles along a seafront, orchards behind them all the way to distant mountains.

"This one's mine," she said, pointing. She said it was wonderful waking to the ocean each morning, like waking to a wealth of possibility.

I had to restrain the bitterness in my voice.

"You said you were going to the centre. Where was it?"

"I did, didn't I? But there isn't one, not in the way I meant. Or it's

9

anywhere. It depends what you're looking for."

"And what were you looking for?"

"I was never sure. But I soon learned I'd never find it in Europe. Everything's haunted by Freud here. If I'd have stayed I'd have spent my whole time looking at pain and breakdown, inventing disciplines of toleration and endurance, finding ways to live more easily with pain. It's nonsense, all that trying to find solace for the past. It's different in the States. We look outward. Change is expected, so it's made to happen. You can believe there'll be something new."

"And what might that be?"

"That's a familiar tone," she said, smiling, "It's always the same here when you mention that one word — new. All the gloom comes out, and pretends it's scepticism."

"Perhaps. Anyway, where's your place in all this change?"

"A few years ago a new chemical was discovered in the brain. It's the only real cause of pleasure. Where I work we're trying to extract the chemical and analyse it. We hope to be able to duplicate it, to produce it artificially, outside the body."

"You're not even a chemist, though."

"No. I was trained the old way. Sometimes I feel years behind. But it's the implications that interest me. I gave up a long time ago the idea that you can inspect the mind in isolation. You've got to look at the mind and body together, as a unit, and treat it as a unit."

"So you'll manufacture this stuff, and then feed it to people like a drug?"

"You're imagining it wrongly, Harry. It's not a drug. It could replace lots of the old tranquilising, inhibiting, depressing things we use now. It won't distort or confuse. It'll allow people to forget their habits of pain, and get into habits of pleasure. Anyway, it's a long way off, and it's not really the point. The work I'm doing is right out on the fringes."

"Oh, so there is a centre?"

She looked at me sharply, then laughed, accepted the irony.

"Yes, I suppose there is. It's still an idea more than anything. But people are getting closer to it, and closer to making it work."

I said nothing. Waiting for her to continue, I poured the last of the champagne into our glasses. She sipped it absent-mindedly, as if in deep thought. When she began talking again, her voice was heavy with American, a transatlantic stream of rhetoric.

"Harry, what would you do if somebody came to you and said, I've found the mechanism in man that makes him violent. I know how to change that mechanism, so that man may become less violent. What should I do? No, you wouldn't know *how* to answer such a question. At the

10

moment, it's so far outside the normal terms of reference that even to ask such a question seems preposterous, something to pour scorn on. But it's the kind of question that *will* be asked, not too far in the future, and if our violence doesn't finish us off in the meantime. It's the kind of question we have to begin to prepare ourselves for. Because, believe me, we will know how to adjust man's mechanisms, how to change his chemical structure in order to change his behaviour. And then we'll really have to think about what we mean when we talk about body and mind, psyche, human nature — all the old phrases that have served us until now."

She leaned forward, searching my eyes for a response. I didn't know what she wanted. All I knew was that her world was impossibly distant from mine, and how strange it was that our two worlds should hang in such precarious balance in this tiny room high above the city. I wanted to stifle her words, to be angry with her, to recriminate and scorn, but I also wanted to draw her close to me, hold her tight in my arms. I said,

"What you're saying is, you can perfect all our imperfections, and at last everything will be find."

"Not quite. Though we will offer a new way to *think* about perfection again. We can at least make it seem a possibility again. At the moment, perfection seems such an *im*possibility, we just fling up our hands in despair. We disbelieve everything, we believe nothing. We go through decade after decade of gloom — the old European, Freudian gloom that squats over our endless discussions of psychic processes, history, human behaviour, political structures, that allows us to see nothing but our unbreakable attachment to a savage past. We see gloom and savagery in our past, we see them in our present, so what can we do but see them in our future also? We expect nothing fundamentally to change. Whatever we talk about, whatever we intend, we go on making the same history, we go on with our savagery and our gloom. All we do is to find new compensations for ourselves, new ways of containing our imperfections. Society itself is nothing but the barrier against its own imperfections. It's pathetic, Harry. There's no optimism, no joy."

"So the biochemists of California will lead us into a new tomorrow.

"Harry, what's at the heart of everything? The individual, the single human organism. Whatever's gone wrong in the world, that's where it must have started. That's where we have to look. That's where we have at least to *consider* making some changes. Who knows, we might end up by refusing to make them, but we have to consider them."

I felt disappointed, cheated even, that she should have returned with this irrational mixture of romanticism, materialism, despair. She didn't even sound convinced by it. Though her speech was filled with her old yearning, it seemed learned, or rehearsed, and when she looked at me, searching for some kind of understanding, approval or consent, I wondered which of us she was trying to persuade. I felt the need to console her. Perhaps wrongly, I imagined she felt she had failed, that although she had found her centre, it continued to elude her. She was still on the fringes, lacking not only the knowledge, but the temperament, the faith, the committment that would take her to the core.

I said, "It seems, I don't know, interesting. I can see how it might excite you."

"You think it's nonsense."

"No. I'm sure it'll come. Once man finds out how to do something, then he does it. It's always been the same. But you must see that it'll involve more than just a bright new future."

She sighed, leaned back in the chair.

"Yes. And of course you're right to be wary."

"I mean, even the words you use, and the way you say them, come from a totally different world from the world they propose."

"I know all that, yes. Thanks for listening, anyway."

"No, I know how important it is, or will be. I could talk about it all night, but..."

"It's okay, Harry. I'm sorry." She closed her eyes tight, raised her hand as if to call me to a halt. "Sometimes I lose sight of myself."

Her enthusiasm was gone. She seemed exhausted, all talked out. She slumped in the chair, her glass balanced on her palm. We sat silent, as if we were waiting. There seemed nothing more to say.

It was past midnight. I went to the window. From far below came the noise of late traffic, of a few ferocious drunks. Street lights stretched away, beyond the river, as far as Durham's distant dark hillsides. Across the stars travelled solitary spots of light.

"It's late," I said, "It's been a strange day."

"For both of us, yes."

"What time do you leave?"

"I fly at eight."

I turned to her, caught her gazing at me. And her name, from all knowledge, understanding or constraint, suddenly broke free.

"Oh Elise."

Undressing, we stripped away everything; everything with which we had burdened ourselves since we had been an adolescent pair holding each other beneath hedgerows, sheltering in shallow depressions in the fields. Illuminated by a square of stars, in that bare rectangular room, we once more learned the newness of each other, and took each other to a world that wasn't some balance of our lived worlds, but that was separate from them, and lay at the limits of touch and desire. It was the only world we could share, and in it we could say anything, the most absurd of things, and let the other hear them.

"Oh Elise I've tried everything, but you go on being in me, in me, part of me. You were everything, all I've ever needed. Oh Elise what can I do to forget you?"

"You were the only one, Harry. Always the only one, still the only one."

"Elise hold me tight. Why did you ever go?"

"You let me, Harry. Why did you let me go? Come into me again. Yes, now. Oh Harry."

Until that was all exhausted, too, and that was all talked out, and all that was left was sleep, and dreams of her.

I woke in the tangled bed, the bare room, sunlight streaming in on me. The smell of Elise was everywhere, but Elise was gone. I lifted her hurried note from the chair.

Harry I did try to wake you.

And I hate goodbyes.

Take care.

    Elise.

It was cold. I dressed quickly, took the lift, walked out of the hotel. Already the sun was high over the rooftops. The city had begun to roar. I told myself, she came for a while, and then she went away again, as she said she would; that's all, nothing more.

Joffy

"Nnnn...nnn...ooo...nnnooot...nnnoott...en...enn..."

"Not enough? That's what you're saying, Joffy?"

"Yyyy...yy..."

The cleaver came down again, cutting away more from the red wedge of meat between the butcher's hands. Joffy, his head level with the marble slab, watched the pile of cubes before his eyes grow.

"How much more, Joffy? Your mammy only wrote steak."

Joffy held the meat between his hands, then held his head in the same way.

"As big as your head," his mother had said, sending him out, "Get enough steak that would fill up your head."

Faced with the meat now, though, he couldn't tell how much that was — it could be squashed, it fell into a sunken heap, but his head had its own hard shape. He looked up at the butcher, Mr McCaufrey, the only man who came to see them now, the only person, apart from those who came to pry and ask questions. Mr McCaufrey waited patiently, as usual, smiling, his face red as the blood on his broad hands, but this was too hard for Joffy. There was nowhere to begin. His tongue squirmed uselessly between his teeth.

"Tell you what, Joffy. You take this, and if you need more, you can come back for it. Okay?"

Walking the hill out of the village, Joffy could feel the meat sliding beneath the pressure of his fingers. He watched blood collect in the corners of the white plastic bag. He knew it didn't matter if there was too little or too much. She was angry anyway, and all yesterday, all this morning, had been shouting at him.

"The cow better not start nosing about again," she said, her mouth twisted, scornful, "She's just like the rest of us underneath it all, thinks her money gives her some right, but it doesn't."

The cow was Auntie Eileen. She was coming today, Saturday, to spoil it. Saturdays he liked to be alone. His mother went out, not to return until the next morning, telling him he must stay near the house, go no further than the garden. He went to the quarry, sat by the pond there, that had begun to be packed with frogs now that spring was on its way. He played with them, until darkness came near, then ran quickly home, trembling with anticipation.

But today he would have to stay with them, his mother and his aunt. Auntie Eileen had been before, and he hated her, was frightened by her. She wouldn't just leave him like most other people did, but was always wanting to touch him, fingering his skin, stroking his hair. Hardly anybody else did that. Hardly anybody else could. She always wanted to talk to him, kept asking him questions, telling him if he took his time he could say anything he wanted to. And she wore a fur hat and a fur scarf, even indoors. A fur scarf with animals' heads on its ends that hung down over her shoulders. She would pull him tightly to her huge soft chest, and he would have to stare into the animals' bright empty eyes.

He approached his home, the last house in the village, tiny bungalow isolated by high hawthorn hedges. Beyond it more hawthorn that edged the quarry, and link chain fences to keep the children out, because of falling stones. And far beyond the quarry the town where his school was, to which he travelled in what even his mother called the dooley bus. He hated entering the town in it, trying not to see the grinning bestial faces outside, put on to echo or provoke those inside.

Last time she was here, Auntie Eileen told his mother she should move from here, back into town, where there would be work for her, where Joffy could be close to school.

"We like it here, don't we, Joffy," his mother said, "We can keep ourselves to ourselves. It's fine, and there's plenty space for him."

"Is it enough, though? There's hardly another child in the whole place. The boy needs friends, someone to be with, company."

"Ha!"

Auntie Eileen turned to him, told him to say for himself that he would like friends, but he didn't know how to answer that. When she had gone, his mother, her fists full of five pound notes, muttered angrily all evening, more to the walls than to Joffy,

"Old bag, what does she know? Never had a cock in her whole life but tries to tell me what to do."

Inside were the unfamiliar smells of disinfectant and polish. The living room was cleared of its piles of clothes, of its empty wine bottles. His mother was on the arm of a chair, still in her nightgown, putting on make up before a small hand mirror. He held out the meat to her, but she waved it away in disgust, told him to leave it on the table. She smelt warm, newly-bathed, and he went close to her, pressed himself to her. Sometimes she opened the gown, wrapped him inside it, but not today. With a long coloured fingernail she pushed him away from her, and as he left shouted after him,

"And mind you keep your trap shut today. You say nothing, not about anything. Right?"

She waited,

"Right?"

He turned, biting his lip, nodded.

15

White, tiny-headed, half-dumb Joffy. Into the hedge he went, to his damp dark nest of hollowed earth, broken branches, bark worn smooth by his so much sitting there. Joffy white as a hawthorn petal, coloured only by sparse traceries of pink, pink eyes and his mouth when opened wide as red as any meat. He refused to look at himself now. He had long ago taught himself the horror of himself in mirrors, how he would peer out like some blanched fish used only to deep darkness. And fish-mouthed also, gulping silence.

Only on Saturday nights could he change. With her gone he opened wide the door to her room, sat by her mirrors, spreading his face with her blacks, reds, greens, blues, made himself another Joffy that could glare out from the glass, run unrestrained and naked through the rooms, kicking walls, leaping from chair to chair, yelling his own invented words of savagery or hate. Then slept, in her bed, exhausted and smiling, travelling lucid jungles of colour and noise.

Sunday afternoons she returned, to the silent house, her made bed, Joffy peering at her, white and frightened from his nest.

"Joffy!"

She was calling him, standing in the doorway, in a skirt and a blouse buttoned to her throat, the remains of a cigarette dangling from her fingers.

"Out of there!"

Slapping his face as he came to her, calling him rat, yanking at his muddied trousers, pulling him in by his tangled hair.

"In here. Now. Look at you."

She stripped him in the living room, cleaned him with licked tissues, dressed him in clothes bought yesterday, yellow jeans whose hems had to be turned up around his skinny ankles, shirt of pastel checks, running shoes, brushed his hair so fiercely close to his scalp he was certain the bristles came right through skin, scraped bone.

"Sit there. And dare move!"

He sat at the laid table's edge, gripping a knife blade so tightly his knuckles were white against his white, pressed to tears by his pain, her anger, his wildness that raced impotently beneath his skin and threw into his head pictures of animals' eyes, splashed frogs, carcasses hanging high behind opened white doors. But all that solved so easily when she came to him a half-hour later, sat him in her lap, tolerated his hands seeking her flesh beneath her blouse, his cheek pressed against her hair, whispered to him that he must be good this afternoon, good for her, and folded her arms about him, murmured,

"Little whiteness. My funny little whiteness."

He was good, sat on the floor between them while they faced each other across the hearth. Auntie Eileen had seen his report from school. "Jonathan likes art, and is good at it," it said.

"Oh, Jonathan. Good boy," she said, "You must do some pictures for me."

Crayons gripped in his fists he made furious tangles of colour for her, pressing so hard he gouged the edges of his paper to rags, spread flakes of wax across the floor. She wanted more, though, said,

"Oh, Jonathan, how lovely. You must tell me about it. I think I can see a dog there. And is this a house? Come and tell me."

Waiting, without the animals' heads today, but her own head like a strange birds', her eyes split by half-lens glasses, encouraging him, but Joffy unable to form answers for her, unable to think even of the beginnings of answers for her, his head seething with hatred for her. He simply nodded when she asked if what she saw there was there. He felt sick, the steak as big as his head, that she had cut into tiny pieces for him at lunch, resting like stones inside him, and he wanted only to be away from them, in the quarry, or lying asleep and coloured in his mother's bed.

When the women spoke with each other, it was as if they believed that because he couldn't speak properly, he couldn't hear properly either. At the table it had been all the old things, how they should move from here, go back to town, stop being so cut off, how being here wasn't enough for the boy and was too much for his mother. His mother kept saying they managed, they liked it, it had been hell before they came here and was so much better now.

"But what future is there here?" Auntie Eileen said, "How can they boy improve? How can you get pulled together again? Look at you. You're not the girl you were. Look at that poor lonely boy. You're just eating each other up."

Until his mother could stand it no longer, angrily began to clear the table of dishes and unfinished meat, shouted,

"It's my life, my home, my boy. Fucking leave it like that!"

Joffy had only vague recollections of hell. Of standing spread-eagled on windowsills gazing far down to roaring city streets, of gripping his mother's loose hands in rattling liftshafts, echoing stairwells. He remembered the ache of her long absences, when he was shut alone behind his locked door with the huge distances below, his dreams of falling and his mother's howls, waking next day to find unknown hollow-eyed men repelled by his presence in his mother's arms. Hell had diminished now, was at a distance, in his journeys to school, her anger, the questioning of strangers. Nearer at hand were the comforts of his nest, the damp quarry, his mother's regular presence, the opportunity of pressing himself against her skin, his dense dreams. He wanted to stay here.

"You could find yourself a little job," said Auntie Eileen, "Nothing special, but something to hold body and soul together. And there are so many nice flats now. We'd all help, Elisabeth. It needn't be like it was."

"How do you know how it was?"

"All that's past now, Elisabeth. It's different now. All we want is the best for you. And for Jonathan."

"And for you, for your guilt. Christ when I think of you all then. You didn't give a shit what might happen."

"Oh Elisabeth, can't we let what's past be past? Can't you stop resisting? You could change your whole life, make it so much better for you both. You could meet someone, someone to share your lives with, but what chance have you of that here?"

"Meet someone? A fine catch we'd make. A worn-out twenty-five year old whore and her idiot child. Sure, they'd be falling over themselves to get us."

"Oh, Elisabeth."

"It's true. Look at us. You said it."

"Right from the start we said how it might turn out, but you were so reckless, so determined to go on with it. As soon as you decided you wanted the child you took the chance of all this happening. But now that it has happened you can't just ignore all your responsibilities, you can't just hide and hope they'll go away."

"You're all the same. You, social workers, those buggers at the school. How am I treating him, am I doing right, is this the way to live? Everything about *him*, worrying about *him*. How do you know what it's like, having him here all the time, something that came out of you and you can't get rid of."

"He's your child, Elisabeth. The child you wanted."

"Yes, I wanted the child, but I didn't want *him*."

"You don't mean that."

"Don't I? Sometimes I want to hurt him so much that you won't be able to leave him with me, but you'll have to take him away from me, and leave me alone, let me be myself again, and not just the idiot who got knocked up with her first fuck."

They were silent then. His mother pressed her face to her fists. Auntie Eileen leaned forward, laid her palm on his skull. Joffy searched his dreams, that even in daytime could be more real than his diminished hell, and found one. Sitting surrounded by failing light and his name repeated over and over, he dashed through the tangles of himself to a shallow pond at his centre. He found frogs there, lifted them from the

18

water, packed them in white plastic, dashed them against rocks. In his head and on his paper red mingled fiercely with green, until he exhausted himself, and slept, on swampy ground, feeling water seep through his thin new clothes, dreaming a deeper Joffy, a fleshy mud-burrowing creature, a worm, an eel, a dark Joffy sucking the dark.

"Joffy."

His mother's voice, calmer now, soothing, extracting him from sleep.

"Sleepyhead, come on."

Darkness, the windows dark pink patches of sky and black tips of hedges. Her hands under his armpits and her mouth pressed close to him, whispering. Auntie Eileen standing there, her smile cracked even in the dark. Lifted up to find his mother with his coat, manipulating him into it, saying he would be fine, fine. Lifted again, higher, into Auntie Eileen's arms, pressed to her chest, and she laughed, saying how small he was, how frail. She carried him out into the dusk, his mother opening the door and the garden gate for them, then leaning down to unlock the car door, opening that. Together they lowered him through it, began fastening a belt about his chest, fumbling with the buckle at his waist.

"Mammy!"

After the surprised pause, his mother soothing him again.

"Joffy don't worry it'll be allright. You're going away for a few days to Auntie Eileen's, that's all. Then I'll come for you and never again leave you. We'll go together to somewhere new and never come here again, and everything will be better again, better than it's ever been. Joffy are you listening? Do you understand? Soon everything will be fine. Oh, Joffy it'll be heaven. Be good for me, be good."

"Every day I'll take you somewhere in the car," said Auntie Eileen, "You just choose somewhere, Jonathan, and we'll go there. What do you say to that? Won't it be wonderful?"

Joffy said nothing, knew only that he would not go. He pulled away the belt, squirmed from their grip, ran back into the house and did not stop running until he had stooped through his nest, scrambled through hedges, pulled himself over the link chain fence, skidded on his backside over the rubble and waste at the quarry's edge, struggled through the bracken and bramble on the quarry's floor, and came finally to the pond, a thin slick of water from which the exposed stone rose in a vertical wall. Then he rested, crouched in the undergrowth, licking his torn skin, tasting his blood. No noise but his breathing, his rapid heartbeat, far-off traffic, small animals scratching the weeds. Nothing to see but the water's glistening, branches and the quarry's rim against the sky, a few pale stars, and his hands when he lifted them, their white bloom.

For minutes, nothing but that. Then they came, only their voices at first, calling him from the direction of the house, until he saw their black outlines above him, one on each side of him, travelling the quarry's edge, until over his head they met, by now his mother furious.

"Joffy you're in there! Get out of it! Come on, out!"

She threatened him, that she would flay his hide, that the police would come, that someone would come to take him away for ever from her. He moved only to settle himself closer to the earth, to lift his coat over his head. In the blackness he tried to remove himself from his hearing, from her noise.

"The rats'll get you. The snakes'll crawl all over you. There's a man in those bushes waiting to strangle you."

It was all he found, a night in himself echoing with her words.

"Right. Stay there. Stay all night. Stay for ever. I'm well rid of you. Don't ever come back!"

The voices stopped. Footsteps left him.

Never before except in dreams had he been here at night. He went to the stone and stood with his back to it, staring out of himself, holding rocks in his hands, ready to fling them at any of the horrors predicted by his mother. He felt exposed, white skin glowing in the quarry's black, so smothered his hands in mud, spread his face with it. Dead still again, too scared to blink even, he stood, while the moon lifted itself into the sky, picked out black incomprehensible shadows from the black. Anything could be seen now, any arrangement of hooves, horns and tails, the glint of eyes staring back at him, heads high and misshapen as piled stones, impossible birds ready to fall from shrubs. He wanted to disappear, to be anything but the focus of all this, to be plant, water, soil, stone, anything but Joffy, but it was an age that he stood there being Joffy, Joffy, Joffy.

"Joffy!"

A man's voice, from the quarry's entrance, reassuring him, searching him out.

"Joffy where are you lad? Make a noise and I'll come for you. Don't worry, everything's fine. Come on, Joffy, make a noise."

Joffy crawled towards the voice, saw the man outlined between fence posts against the sky, behind him the still figures of the two women.

"Joffy it's me, Mr McCaufrey. Come on, I'll help you out."

The butcher stepped down, onto the waste, became a hardly-distinguishable descending shadow, florid face lost among so much dark. On the quarry floor, he was noise, the snapping of twigs and stems, a gross blundering body calling, "Joffy, Joffy, Joffy." And Joffy grinned, knowing himself dominant, knowing this place, knowing himself small, mud-covered, silent. It was easy to roll unnoticed from the butcher's clumsiness. Easy to go on grinning, snigger when the butcher finally called to the women that it was hopeless, that he could see nothing, that maybe the boy wasn't there anyway, and began to make his way out of the quarry towards them. And when he was once more visible against the sky, it was easy for Joffy to allow his sniggering to rise in pitch and loudness, to become a wild piercing noise ringing from the dark to the adults high above.

When he had calmed, they were gone, leaving him to stay, he supposed, as his mother had said, for ever. He stood up, picked his way over the waste, climbed the fence, stood watching. Through the hedges shone the village lights, nearest to him those of his home. He went towards them, came to his nest, saw from there the adults inside talking, shaking their heads. He stood at the window, heard his mother sure he would return. They should go, she said, or he'd stay out there all night. She would call for the butcher if he were needed. Auntie Eileen should come back another day, when they'd try again. The butcher and Auntie Eileen left. Over the rooftops Joffy heard the car starting, the butcher's heels on the pavement, subdued farewells. Joffy laughed, and remained standing there, knowing he would not be seen, when his mother came to stare out between her hands into the night. When she came out, he pressed himself close to the wall, allowed her to pass within inches of him. She crouched at his nest, pulled branches and weeds aside, cursed him.

Grinning, he went into the house, stood by the fireside, waiting.

She said nothing. Everything seemed long prepared for. Hardly looking at him, she took his arm, led him to the bathroom where she undressed and bathed him, dried him with coarse towels that left his skin stinging. He showed no sign of complaint. Nothing seemed required of him. She took him to his room, pulled aside the covers on his bed, laid him face down on it.

"I'll tame you, boy," she said, her voice now drained of anger and scorn.

She took a belt from her waist, pinned his neck to the bed with her free hand, and beat him until he could be silent no longer but protested, screamed, as flesh burst his skin and became meat. He tried to thrash away from the pain, but there was no release until he abandoned himself to it, allowed it to fall into him, covering him over, leaving him finally insensitive in a dark silence where there was nothing, no Joffy at all.

Hours of dreamless sleep had passed when he opened his eyes, found himself standing outside his tangled bed. He walked like Joffy always wanted to walk, erect, his head high.

Outside her window stars, as far away as pain, clustered thickly about the moon's ring. From her mirror's rim, light shone on him, on his white face, white as petals, paper, snow, as everything that had ever been white. White as the absence of all dark, of any hint of shade. He changed it, with her lipsticks, creams and powders made another Joffy's face, striped, spotted, starred, a rain of glistening dust falling across its surface. And mascaraed his hair into a stiff mane, black as night.

He stood over her waiting, but there was only her breathing, her eyes flickering violently beneath their lids.

"Mammy," he said, "Mammy."

Even before she was fully awake, she was smiling at him, gazing far into him, and he felt himself being filled with her, so that there was no room for anything but her.

"Mammy, let me in."

She lifted the bedclothes, drew him towards her, held him close to her.

"Mammy, let me stay," he said, and all night, as if for ever, his peculiarly coloured features roamed her white skin.

Concentric Rings

This story is not mine. It was told to me by one of our many street performers, an acrobat who had specialised in spinning. Even in old age, at a time when he should be staggering towards death, or already lie rotting in his grave, he described intricate loops and spirals across the open areas of the city. They were astonishing performances, of an unnatural vigour, but they were also a deterioration, for it was said that in youth his spinning had been so rapid as to take him to the very edge of invisibility.

Though, whenever he passed by my desk in the bazzar, we called out polite greetings to each other, I had never spoken with him, and had come to believe that his reserve was the outcome of his contempt for my sedentary occupation. One morning, however, I looked up from my work to find him standing before me. He had lifted from the corner of my desk an object I had thrown there in frustration. He was fingering it, gazing at it as if at some reawakened memory.

I had found it the previous evening, in the course of clearing out my father's chests. It consisted of a pair of concentric rings, the inner leather ring being attached to a metal ring by a system of radiating springs. The inner ring was buckled, so that like a belt it could be expanded or contracted. My father had entered the long unconsciousness that was to precede his death, so he was unable to guide my understanding of it. I had cleaned it, oiled it, so that the buckle and springs had loosened, and it seemed to have regained its potential. But I could imagine no purpose for it. Was it a trap, the remains of some obscure engine or machine, an instrument of torture? The solutions which seemed most probable were an irritation, for I knew that I might accept as true a solution that bore no relation to the real truth. I had given up my private speculations, saw that they would have to be tested against the knowledge of someone else.

"Do you know what it is?" I asked.

Of course. Though I thought it had been burned with the rest. Do you not know?"

"No." I told him how I had come across it, and he laughed.

"Yes, he would want to keep some part of it," he said, "He was always sitting there, taking note. He missed nothing."

"He's dying."

"Yes, I heard. Still, I can see he's prepared you well."

"He can't help me with this."

"This? It'll tell you nothing about him."

"I'm not interested in that. If you can tell me what it is, then do. I don't need a long explanation. It needn't take long."

"It's not that easy."

He looked about him. The bazaar was already filled with people, a potential audience.

"I should be working," he said.

I invited him to sit in the chair beside me, where for years my father had sat, training me. He laughed again, and said I was truly my father's son, but then shrugged, and sat there. For minutes, he was silent, ordering his memories, before he began.

"I'm an acrobat. I've always been one, like my father, like my father's father. It's my obsession and my life. I *am* that obsession, nothing more. I've spent all my energy on it, on becoming, and remaining, the finest acrobat, the greatest spinning man, that this city's ever seen. I'm going to fail, of course. Better than anyone I know how poor my performances are now, if I compare them with those of my youth. But what of it? Should I despair? No, even I, who try to oppose time, have to accept that we're all subject to it. Otherwise obsession would become madness, wouldn't it? I'm telling you this so that you'll understand that in order to become what I've become, I haven't been able to live like others do. For me, life is a constant training for performance. It's a constant spinning, that only death will trip. The way I live cuts me off. It means that even though I live in a city packed with people, with people who watch me and applaud me, I can't live as they do. How can I? I see them, when they turn away after my performances, turn to a life of trivia, to a quest for futile pleasures, novelties. I'm not condemning them. I can even imagine the attractions of their lives, but I can't, because of my obsession, follow them. Anyway, beause of all that, *I've* become a spectator, watching the life of a city that can't involve me. A poor spectator, certainly, because I've seen little to intrigue me, little to catch my attention, even. But this morning, looking at these rings, I'm reminded of a time when an obsession as strong as my own gripped the lives of many of the people around me. I watched the obsession grow, saw in it my own purpose of opposing time, of opposing death itself. Most intriguing of all, I watched an obsession that was *shared*, that contrasted vividly with my own isolation."

He was silent again. I feared that the frustrations of sitting, of controlling words rather than movements would cause him to leave me. But he seemed to have forgotten his surroundings and his spectators, to be lost in himself, until the beginning of his story suddenly showed itself to him, and led him inexorably towards its end.

"How can I say it started? A woman came to the city. Who she was or where she came from we never knew. How could we? She spoke in grunts, like some animal. Some people said they could hear patterns in her grunts that must have meaning, that she was speaking some language. If it was language, it wasn't one that even our most-travelled merchants had come across, and no-one ever showed any sign of understanding it. Neither did she learn anything of ours. When we asked, "Where did you come from?" and pointed inquiringly in several directions, she nodded vigorously, agreed that she came from all directions.

"I say she was a woman. And she was, I suppose, or the core of her was. But she was a woman changed into a beast of burden. The first time she was seen was when she came through the gates. She was tied between the shafts of a cart by ropes and belts that had cut deep sores into her flesh. She was leaning forward, almost on all fours. Sweat, and blood from her wounds ran from her into the mud. When she got as far as the market-place, she unloosened herself and fell down in a faint. Nobody went to help her. Some of the stallkeepers inspected her cart— there were bundles of torn clothes, a few animal skins, boxes of bruised vegetables. They turned away in contempt. It seemed as if she was just one more of the inadequates who come here without possessions or gifts, to beg from us, or to sneak out of the shadows to grab satisfaction for their envies and their needs. She would have been left there, but when she recovered she started to unload her belongings, and arranged them like makeshift furniture, as if she was setting up home there. It enraged the stallkeepers. They threw her things back into the cart, pushed her back between the shafts, told her to get out. She was like a nervous animal at first, dodging their blows, trembling, with a wild terror in her eyes. But that didn't last long. Her nervousness suddenly became rage and she fought back with a strength unseen in any other woman. It wasn't so much her strength that made them scatter, as the wild bestial howling with which she accompanied it— a sickening sound, evil, as if a demon was snarling from beneath her flesh.

"All this time I'd been working, but the noise had drawn away my spectators one by one, and I was left performing in front of a few drunkards. I went to see what was happening. By the time I arrived, and had slipped through to the front of the crowd, she had fixed up a ragged tent and was removing the last few boxes from the cart. Until she came to the last one, she threw them down carelessly, spilling their conents to the ground, but that last one she lifted as if it contained everything precious. She sat down cross-legged in the dirt, lifted a roll of sheepskin from the box, unrolled the sheepskin in her lap, and took out her child from it.

"Her child. I'd seen nothing like it. It was a boy, that's all we could be sure of, but the strangest boy I'd ever seen. He had a head as big as a man's, as big as ours are. Except for a few pale hairs for eyebrows it was completely hairless. His features were tiny, like tiny engravings on his skin, and his eyes, the palest, most watery blue eyes, were completely expressionless. That head seemed to be all of him that mattered. Beneath it was a body that was shrunken or had failed to grow. Usually, the body supports the head. In him, it was as if the body hung down from the head, was nothing but an attachment. He hardly had shoulders at all. The limbs were small and stunted, folded up as if they had never been used.

"Such an odd contrast they made, that pair. Such a child sitting on such a woman's lap. When she looked at us now, there was a trace of conquest in her eyes, and I remember thinking, when she lifted him to her breast and began to suckle him, how like a performer she seemed, knowing that she had stirred our interest, delighting in the knowledge that we were at once fascinated and repelled.

"I don't know. Maybe she was just a performer and nothing more. Maybe the whole thing was just a trick she had developed, a way of turning their handicaps into advantages, of gaining favour and charity wherever she went. Whatever it was, it was enough to turn part of this city mad.

"Early the next day, soon after dawn, I came up here as usual to practise before the crowds came. But what I saw, next to her tent, was enough to destroy any thought of work. The back of her cart was staked to the ground, so that the shafts were tilted high. From one of the shafts hung a rope, and on the end of the rope, a noose about his neck, was the boy, turning slow circles in the breeze. I rushed towards him, yelling curses at his mother and at those who stood beneath him watching. I was about to leap up to him, to unfasten him, but someone held me back and said,

"Look. He's smiling."

And he was. He was looking down and smiling.

"When I had recovered from my first surprise, and began to look closely at the boy, it seemed clear enough what was happening. Where his voice box should have been there was a pad of muscle, a continuation of the muscles at the sides and back of his neck. These muscles were so highly developed that they made an unbroken ring protecting his breathing passages. That, and the unnaturally light weight of his body, meant that the rope couldn't strangle him.

"As I say, it seemed clear enough, but you know what we're like here. Soon there were dozens of us standing there watching, and the most nonsensical theories about the boy's abilities began to be passed around—most of them based on the supposed supernatural powers of the boy, of his mother, or of both of them together. Anybody who put forward a more rational explanation was immediately ridiculed. Of course the confusion was helped by the fact that whenever the mother was encouraged to enter the debate, all she could contribute were her grunts.

"Like a good entertainer, she knew how to keep us there. All morning she kept lifting the boy out of his noose, showing him to us, allowing those who dared to touch him, before tightening once more the rope around his neck. Each time she pushed him away from her a wave of horror and delight rushed through us. By afternoon, though, some people began to get bored with it– after all, it was just the same thing over and over. And people started to leave, either because of the boredom, or because they were tired of having their reasoning mocked. As the sun was going down she unfastened him for the last time, and began suckling him again, all the time murmuring gently into his ear. He kept lifting his head from her breast and looking at her. He made tiny mewing noises, like a small cat.

"I realised then that I'd gone a whole day without working. It made me angry, especially when I looked around and saw that I was one of the last few people left. Somehow we'd drawn closer and closer to the woman and her child, and we were crouched in a half-circle in front of them. I stood up quickly and went home. I must have been the last to leave, because next morning the others were still there, sleeping uncomfortably in the dirt.

"It was as if that first day had been a time for testing us out, for trimming down the audience to a core of true believers. Because after that she showed no interest in anyone except the ones who had stayed all night. She sat among them, passed the boy among them. At first they were just looking closely at him and inspecting him with their fingers, but pretty soon they began to nuzzle him, kiss him, press him close to their hearts. It was sickening, disgusting really, seeing how quickly grown people, men and women, had allowed themselves to be entranced by that grotesque pair. But we've seen a lot worse things here, and most of the rest of us just wanted to leave them to it and get on with our own lives. But that wasn't easy, because there they were, in the marketplace. They improved her tent for her, brought her food and clothing. They made the boy a manger, lined it with the finest and softest cloths. They brought their own bedding, set up their homes there. In all of this they seemed untouched by all the entreaties of their friends and families. The space beside the woman's cart became a strange encampment, right in the centre of the city.

"Though they were there at the centre, it was as if they'd left all of the rest of us behind, as if they were going to something they'd waited their whole lives for. But what were they going to? An idiot mother and her idiot child. How do you explain something like that? It's like there's something missing from some people, isn't it? Most times they don't even know it. They just know they're discontented. They can't make their own lives be enough for them. There's a huge gap in them. They cover it over by working, by watching people like me, by seeking out novelties, by just continuing until they can't continue any more. Then they die, discontented as ever. But sometimes something happens, they see something, they hear something, something that makes them stop makes them think about themselves and about what's missing. That should be a good thing, shouldn't it? It should show them how to change things, to make them better.

"It should. But it never happens like that. I've never seen it happen like that. I don't know why, but it always goes wrong somehow, sometimes its wrong right from the start. Sometimes the wrong something happens, or they see it wrongly, hear it wrongly, get the wrong meaning from it. So it's no wonder the changes they make are the wrong ones. Sometimes it doesn't matter too much – they just exchange one false life for another. But sometimes it does. I've seen people give up everything to follow a dream or an idea that they think will solve everything, but that can only lead them to their own destruction. It's a kind of madness, but that seems to be the only thing some people can find to fill up the gap in themselves – madness.

"Anyway, that's what happened to those people. They turned mad, mad in what they said, and then mad in what they did. They said the woman and her son had been sent here. They didn't know where from and they didn't know who by. But it was deliberate that they didn't know, in the same way that it was deliberate that she didn't know how to speak to us. That way, the burden of understanding fell on us, and it was a burden, because it needed an effort of will, intelligence, imagination. Anybody who didn't make the effort would continue in their ignorance and cynicism.

"This is what their effort came to – they said that the woman and boy were rich with meaning. The woman, with her muscles and the marks left by years of strain, was a symbol of the body, something tied to the earth, doomed. Her boy was the outward image of the spirit, that in most of us lies dormant, unseen. When he was hanged, he showed that the spirit transcends the body and the earth, that it can defeat death itself.

"Of course there's no harm in talk like that. You can invent meanings for anything if you put your mind to it. Some people spend their whole lives doing little else. But these people went further than that. They said that the boy's shape showed that the spirit is an embryo inside us, that it can be born in each of us as he was born from the body of his mother. Inorder that this could happen, they said that they did not have to abandon the body, that they did not have to die, but that their bodies must be reshaped so that it corresponded more exactly with the shape of the spirit as seen in the boy. In that way, the body and the spirit could be brought to live in harmony, as the mother and her child lived in harmony, that they could become a perfect pair. And in perfection, of course, there's no death. That was their final, and maddest belief – that they could become immortal.

"I keep saying they were mad. They were. But wasn't it just as mad that a few people who believed something like that were surrounded every day by hundreds of other people who knew it was all nonsense, but who could do nothing to make them see that. Some of us did try, certainly, and even managed to persuade a few of them to see sense. The rest resisted everything. Their faith was like a huge wall that nobody would ever get over.

"And the rest of us, who were supposed to be the sane ones, but who did nothing to persuade anyone? I was typical. I knew it was nonsense, but somehow I managed to tell myself that it might not be, and most important of all, I wanted to see what would happen next.

"How do you change the body? It's not too difficult. It changes itself, adapts itself to the way you live. Mine's hard and muscular, because of the way I use it. Look at yours. It's already soft, a little flabby, because you're sitting most of the time, hardly using it at all. But these people wanted a most peculiar shape. They wanted most of their muscle to waste away, ideally to be like the boy's, so shrunken they couldn't even be used. At the same time, they wanted that thick pad of muscle around their throats. It was hardly a natural shape, so it called for a very unnatural discipline.

"These rings were just a fragment of that discipline, of a ludicrous apparatus and way of life that were designed to turn them into copies of the boy. Watch. The rings went over the head, like this, then the inside ring was tightened around the throat. They had chairs made. Above the seat, they could close the chairs around them in a tight tube. The outer metal ring was fixed over the top of the tube. Their legs were fastened to the bottom of the chair by straps. What it all meant was that the only part of the body that could be moved was the neck, and in order to move that, they had to pull against the pressure of the springs. So the whole contraption seemed perfect – it strengthened the neck, and weakened everything else.

"Of course it took a long time to get the chairs made, and it was expensive. Some of them had no trouble in affording it. Others sold their belongings, sometimes everything they owned. The ones who had nothing, neither money nor saleable possessions, tried to make do with imitations of the chair, but they ended up with nothing but awkward parodies of it. They were all in competition with each other. It was as if only the possession of a perfect chair allowed entry to the inner circle of the faithful. So the chair was another test – those who failed it were no longer true believers. They tried to keep their attachment to the faith, but you could see that they were outcasts. Some of them became sickened by their position, and left the encampment altogether, tried to pick up the thread of their old lives again, but most of them stayed, and formed a dejected, rather pathetic group clinging to the fringes of the chairowners.

"At the centre, there were a dozen, who had kept their faith intact, and who had come into possession of a chair. They sat in a tight circle around the mother and her child. They had a brand new scaffold built, and twice each day, at sunrise and sunset, she stepped up to it with her boy in her arms, hanged him from it and pushed him away from herself, while the chairowners whimpered eerie melodies of praise. Though that ritual accentuated how far beyond our influence they had travelled, sometimes it seemed as if the whole city was feeding off them. Not only did we gain a perverse kind of entertainment from them, but a whole network of business and trade was formed around them. Though the boy had been seen to consume nothing but his mother's milk, they came to believe that their progress would be quickened if they ate only the meat of strong-necked beasts. Hearing this, hunters and merchants were forever adding to their heap of carcasses, and asking, and receiving, the most outrageous prices. And I don't think there was one apothecary at that time who didn't invent a cream, a pill or an ointment, and offer it to them as the perfect potion for shape-changing.

"They were employers, too. They hired large muscular men as a protection against the possible aggressions and supplications of heretical citizens. These bodyguards serviced the chairowners' needs. They fed them. They shaved them, at least twice each day, not just their faces but every part of them, so that they could imitate the perfect hairlessness of the boy. At regular intervals the bodyguards lifted them from their chairs, and carried them to latrines where they strained to force out the waste that might infect their purity.

"Living in such a way, it was hardly surprising that they made progress towards their ideal. They had to fit stronger and stronger springs about their necks, loosen the buckles to accommodate their growth. We saw when they were carried from the chairs how shrunken and wasted their other muscles became. Their skin was pale and slack, covered by sores and blemishes. Their faces when they passed by us were spectres, unfocused, staring bleakly at nothingness. Some said it was meditation. It wasn't. They were abandoned faces, drained of life.

"And as their lives drained, so did my germ of hope, of any faith I had somehow continued to imagine. It was finally destroyed when one of them awoke from his madness, tried to retreat from death.

"He had been a house builder in his past life, a vigorous, successful man. Even now you can see the results of his work in many of the city's streets. I don't know, perhaps an image from that past life, perhaps the face of some former friend or lover, found its way into his stillness and suddenly began to haunt him. Anyway, he began screaming – a wordless screaming filled with revulsion, terror. From somewhere he found the strength to fling open his chair as if to leap from it. He fell from it, could hardly hold himself on all fours. He tried to squirm his way out from the circle but his every move was opposed by his own bodyguard, who finally lifted him, thrust him back into the chair. But again he flung open the chair and again fell from it. Several times the act was repeated, until the bodyguard lifted him high into the air and threw him out. Once they realised what was happening, the outcasts, whose progress to perfection, compared with that of the chairowners, had been so slow, began to release themselves from their own contraptions, and scrambled over each other, fighting to gain the vacant chair. Some bystanders, perhaps hoping that this first break in the circle might precipitate an end to the whole affair, rushed forward to restrain them, but they themselves were opposed with such violence by the bodyguards that they were forced to retreat. In the end the chair was again occupied, and the failed outcasts tied themselves up again, muttering their despair.

"We tried to help the one who had been thrown out, but at each touch he cowered, as if in fear of great pain. Broken, deformed and inarticulate, scorned even by those who had once loved him, he lay there for days, a beggar, feeding on the scraps and waste that were thrown at him, until one morning we found him dead.

"To the other chairowners that day, it was as if everything had happened in another world. It had, in a sense. It had happened in the world of the living, while they were entering the world of the dead. That's what it meant now. They had trained themselves into a stillness that wasn't calm or peace, but was a kind of stagnation, a rotting down. Like the rest of us, they had once had everything – a life of body, mind, spirit, but they had stopped using it, had refused to use it. And when life isn't used it just rots down into itself, as surely as the body rots into itself in the grave. That day life had tried to assert itself. It had demanded to be recognised, but it was too late. Even the creature it had asserted itself in was too far gone towards death to be able to do anything about it. Death had the upper hand. It squatted with that woman and that child at the centre of the ring of chairs, and inexorably sucked the owners of the chairs towards it. Already they existed in a kind of living death. At the most, there would perhaps be a few more bursts of violence. Then, soon enough, death would truly come into its own. They would die.

"I saw how mad it had been to hope that it might have ended in any other way. I gave myself completely to my work. I've been told that that was my best ever time. It's true. And it's true of many of the performers who were working then. We had a vigour that was almost desperate, that pressed us towards feats of greater and greater daring. Time and again we found the limits of our energies and skills, but even as we found them we found some means of going beyond them. It was because of the chairowners, of course. There they were, at our heart, and it was impossible to work without catching sight of them. They provoked us, they spun us on. How could we look at death without giving our almost miraculous display of death's opposite?

"Sometimes, because of the effect it had on our performances, I wish that it had lasted longer, that death had claimed them only after years of slow collapse. But it wasn't to be. The greatest work of my life was crammed into a few short weeks. Then the scaffolds were built, a ring of them, one at the back of each chair, a noose hanging down over the head of each owner. The scaffolds were to be the stage upon which they would give their finest performance. Their months of discipline, meditation, had all been direced towards it. The crowds came back, sat for a day waiting while the city was filled with the noise of hammering and sawing. And I joined them. Why were we there? Did we still hope that death could be cheated? Did we believe that the spirit had been caused to flourish in those mutilated bodies? In some faces there were the signs of such hope and faith, it's true. But the rest of us? We had been brought back as we can be brought back by any good entertainer's trick. We had the opportunity to be there at the end of a performance that had intrigued, inspired, bored and horrified us. We didn't want to miss the final flourish.

"The carpenters finished their work, walked away from it. Criticised by anyone, they merely shrugged. It was business, after all. Then there was silence for an hour, everything as normal.

"In the late afternoon, the bodyguards began to open the chairs, to loosen the straps and rings, to replace the rings with the ropes. As if only now understanding what had been so long prepared for, some of the crowd shrieked in protest, and leapt forward in a vain rescue attempt. They were thrown back at us, to begin a desperate sobbing, pierced by guilt.

32

"As usual, when the sun hung low over the walls, the woman lifted her boy and hanged him. He turned a few slow circles, and then, as if at some signal, though I saw none, each bodyguard gripped the free end of his rope and lifted his master from the chair.

"And that was the end of it all. The bodies gave a few last kicks against the madness. Some of them managed a strangled cry of anger or despair. But within a few minutes the only thing that moved them was the breeze, and the slow spinning of the ropes. At last, dead, they were able to give a reasonable imitation of the boy."

At this, the acrobat stretched himself in his chair, arching his back, holding his arms high above his head. He yawned, and turned to me laughing.

"And that's what it had all been for," he said, "It's crazy, isn't it? Telling it all to you now, it's like telling a story. I can hardly believe that something like that really happened, and seemed to matter so much."

"So they all died?" I asked.

"Of course. What else? They all died, and we stood watching, and did nothing."

"What about the boy?"

"Oh, he was fine. Though he wouldn't have been if we could have got to him, nor would his mother, but as usual the bodyguards were in the way, and wouldn't let us near them. She started packing up straight away, put the boy in his box, tied herself to the cart, and set off. The bodyguards, who you could see now were probably more entranced than anyone, followed them. The outcasts went as well, limping, staggering and crawling – I doubt if they ever kept up."

"Then you burned everything?"

"The whole lot. Except this, thanks to your father. We heaped everything up – chairs and scaffolds, the outcasts' contraptions, the meat and all the pills and potions. Then we threw the corpses themselves on top, and set light to it all. By the next morning nothing was left but a ring of smouldering ash."

His story over, he was preparing to leave me, but I wanted to find a way to restrain him, and explore further a past that my father's unconsciousness denied me.

"And the way your work was stimulated then," I said, "Was there no other time that had a similar effect?" But the question irritated him, and seemed to hurry his departure.

"How can I talk about that?" he said, "With work like mine it's a matter of doing it, and talking isn't doing it. Anyway, good effects, bad effects – you take them as they come."

He had withdrawn from me. He shook my hand and left, walking stealthily towards the centre of the bazaar. I tried to return to my own work, but the commissioned letters, the bills of sale and the announcements remained unwritten. Soon I put down my pen and followed him, stood in the crowd that watched him, cheered his skill, gasped at his daring, applauded his deteriorating spinning towards death.

Dark Cube

He was a familiar figure in the bazaar, yet he was known to no one. Each morning from the stalls he bought the simple requirements of life, held conversation with no one, took no interest in our attractions and entertainments, and returned in silence, looking neither to left nor right, to the warren of alleys and passages from which he had come. Greeted by others, he merely dipped his head lower, quickened his step.

Ever eager to speculate and imagine, some said that he must surely be involved in some obscure experimentation or research, to be so unmoved by the life and society of his city. Others scorned this. His aspect of seriousness and deep meditation, they said, was in truth the mask worn by an extreme emptiness and stupidity. He did not react because he had nothing with which to react. Yet others pitied him, saying that he had turned his face from his contemporaries in order to search the darkness in himself, only find himself entangled in the alleyways that would entangle us all, were it not for our grateful participation in our time. Whatever our view, we all agreed that he had little to offer our time, and we learned to tolerate, and to ignore, his voluntary isolation.

The first time that he stayed with us, therefore, it was the fact of his staying, and the fact of his wanting to perform for us, which amazed us, rather than the performance itself, which seemed absurd.

It was evening. Released from the day's burdens, we had come together to be amused, refreshed and entertained. The sun had sunk over the palace, and on the stalls hundreds of tiny, differently-coloured lamps were being lit. Holding before him a small cubical wooden casket from whose joints a light gleamed, he appeared in the space among some tables, and called for those who dined there to attend him. To each group in turn he showed the box, and then to the other intrigued groups who soon came to stand about him, nudging each other and winking their amusement.

It was a bare, unornamented, hinged box. He lifted the lid, and lowered it so that it hung down against one of the sides. Then he released each side and they fell down to hang over his hand, leaving the whole interior of the box exposed. In that interior, supported by the base, was a single candle whose flame flickered uneasily above his trembling arm, and which swayed back and forth as he turned to exhibit it to each section of his audience. All leaned closer, certain that they had been brought together to see more in the box than a single candle and its flame. But they had not. He extinguished the flame, closed the box, moved from the centre of the crowd, and attempted to force his way through the knotted ring of bodies. But of course they resisted him, and started to mock him. Is that all there is? they called. Do you expect to satisfy us with that?

He raised his arm, hushing them.

"See how in darkness," he said, "we see the light."

And with us torn by hilarity, he was able to leave us, with our proven knowledge that he was a fool.

Next day he returned to find that his performance had caused him to become the centre of all attention. Encouraged by their parents, children trailed him as he came out from the alleyways, forming a procession loud with their squealed music and mock praise. Dogs leapt and tore at his cloak. Stallkeepers and purchasers hailed him, demanded more demonstrations of his spectacular skills and learning.

"Bring out your box," they called, "Bring out your box."

Reaching an open space, he turned to his followers, and from a deep pocket did bring out the box. The crowd gasped, imitating awe.

The performance was repeated. The box was exhibited and opened. But this time, as he released the sides, we saw that there was no candle, and to our delight, someone shouted,

"See how in light, we the darkness."

When all sides were released, there appeared to be another box, until now enclosed within the·first. It was perfectly black, with no reflection on its surface, without joints or hinges. He turned, showing it, and we demanded that he open it.

In answer, he went to the stall of a seller of caged birds, and with his free hand brought out the most dazzlingly-coloured bird from its cage. Muttering to it, he allowed it to perch for a moment on his finger, singing, before, without opening hinges or loosening joints, he placed the bird inside the box, so that we could see nothing of it, but could hear its continuing sweet song. Silent, we edged in circles around him, leaning close, searching an opening, a glimpse of the lost bird. But it only appeared when he struck the wooden base, and it dashed out, flying ·wildly to the sky.

This time, as he closed the box, and replaced it among the folds of his heavy garments, we moved aside, allowing him to leave us, and the procession that followed him was hushed, confused. Though at the edge of the bazaar we called after him, "What is it? Explain it. Let us inspect it," he continued in his accustomed way, looking neither to left nor right, his head hung low. And those who trailed him further, and peered through his window and the frame of his door, returned that evening without tales of laboratories, practised illusion or sorcery, but of his sitting in a dark room, meditating, with the box open before him, and his hands lost in the blackness within.

In the weeks that followed, he dispelled all our ignorance. He came back regularly, and showed us all there was to show. We saw that the interior of the wooden box was not another box, but was a perfect cube of darkness that obscured anything that entered it, and no light could dispel. It was a darkness deeper than the darkness of night, for in it candles went on burning, without emitting rays. He beckoned us close to it, and copying him we learned the courage to place our hands there and see them lost even while we could feel them and clench them and know that they were there, until after a time courage was no longer needed and the dark cube became our plaything. We dipped our cheeks and chins in it, making laughably severed heads, or went lower and stared into a darkness that had no visible exit, yet just beyond which were the faces of our grinning friends.

But as with all playthings, boredom was its burden, and again we began to ask, is this all there is? Though he encouraged none of it, and resisted all questioning, we argued among ourselves, many claiming to have divined the true nature and power of his darkness. The lame and the withered were brought, to rest their limbs in it, searching healing Mothers bathed their children in it, as if in some ritual cleansing or benediction. Groups of acolytes formed, who took no part in our play, but at the opening of the box bowed their heads and chanted low murmurous sounds of confession and praise. Others turned away, and warned that an object so negative could only cause dismay and suffering around itself.

Yet the city thrived, as always, and was beset by neither increased blessings nor calamities. The lame continued limping. The withered withered. Children grew as they were due to grow, straight or stilted, luminous or dull. So that finally even those who had imagined its unearthly goodness or malevolence were brought to recognise: the darkness had no power, only its quality of being dark. It was indeed all there was.

Fascination, and his audiences, waned. We shrugged him back to his barren meditations, and he became again the solitary, bowed figure, hurrying out from and into his alleyways, with nothing to communicate or to perform, until one day we realised he was no longer even that. Unseen, he was forgotten, lost in the obscurity of the past.

Only once, years later, were we reminded of him. A group of entertainers erected before us a tall wooden casket on a stage. Opening it, they revealed the masked, heavily cloaked figure of a man. They pulled away the masks and cloaks, and left an unclothed darkness, through which they passed their hands and in which they stood, calling to us. But we were unimpressed. It was an old illusion, by then we had been seduced by other wonders, and darkness in the shape of man was unable to amaze us.

Chickens

Jack watched his grandson walk clumsily through rows of lettuce towards him. For an hour he had sat against the greenhouse wall, in his blue serge suit and cloth cap, facing south. Beyond the shimmering rooftops patches of children had moved across the playing fields to begin their games, their high voices coming to him mingled with the sounds of distant motor cars and factories. Insects had drifted lazily in and out of his hearing and high above a lark incessantly had called its notes. At the sound of the gate's latch he leaned forward expectantly.

The boy came awkwardly, in wellingtons, crunching grit. He picked his way over the flower beds, stripping off his shirt. The old man sat back again.

"Good start to your holidays," he said.

The boy grinned and sat beside him on the bricks that had lain unmoved for years against the glittering building. He leaned at ease against the hot glass, pleased to be surrounded again by the familiar smells of tobacco and earth.

"Peter coming?" asked his grandfather.

Sammy shook his head. Peter was still in bed. Jack grunted, unsurprised, and took out his pocket watch. Almost nine. He rose stiffly and knocked out his pipe against the wooden frame of the building.

"Are the tomatoes ready?" asked Sammy as they went round to the door.

Jack smiled. "No, but there's some late chickens hatched out."

Sammy loved the greenhouse. The door opened into a dark and musty interior, littered with tools and scraps of all kinds. Rusted implements hung from year to year on the walls without being touched. Rat traps, always empty, lay in the corners. He picked his way over the obstacles and opened the door of the greenhouse itself. He entered the sudden heat and breathed the sweet powdery smell of tomatoes. He went to a large cardboard box and put his hand inside, laughing at the tiny voices and the tiny feet scratching his skin. He lifted one of the chicks and held it, bright yellow, to his face, astonished that it would grow into one of the noisy unshapely birds that strutted around the henhouse.

"Can this one be mine?" he asked.

"Aye, that can be yours," said Jack, entering, knowing how much the boy's continued interest in the allotment depended on such pleasures. "Your mam allright?"

Sammy nodded. "She wants a lettuce, if there's any."

"Aye, I've got some flowers for her as well. Come on."

He led the way out and Sammy replaced the bird, hesitating for a moment to see if he could distinguish a single ball of fluff among so many.

Jack was seventy, Sammy ten, Peter twelve. Since the boys had been able to walk the allotment had been a playground for them, their grandfather a strange and regular companion. He had rented the land for thirty years, but it had only really been alive since the boys had come. Peter had been the first, and had long held prime place in the old man's affections. But it was no surprise that Sammy now tended to come alone. For two years a change had been happening, and Jack had watched the elder boy moving into a new world. He was an old man, but recognised the scorn with which Peter performed the simple tasks he had once enjoyed. While regretting this, he had himself undergone a subtle, and largely unconscious change, and it was now Sammy for who he watched and listened. And now he looked on in deep content as the boy crouched in the dirt to cut his mother's lettuce.

The boys were aware that they occupied a privileged position, and that the fierce and exclusive love Jack bore them brought them into contact with an area of his life denied to others. Once Sammy had heard his grandmother complain that nothing affected her husband except the children. And Sammy had wanted to say that she didn't really understand, that she didn't really know him, but even then had realised how absurd such a statement would sound, and had remained silent. To the fatherless boys the old man was a towering figure. A holiday from school seemed inconceivable without his presence, and while Sammy sensed his brother's growing resentment of this, he was still too young to understand the reasons behind it. He accepted and enjoyed Jack, and secretly believed that Peter's new attitudes were not good. Anyway, his grandfather was never less than a source of pleasure. It was he who took them away, to parks and beaches and cinemas, best of all to the pig farm past the playing fields, with its monstrous animals, noises and smells. And it was he who had the allotment, where they could build fires, carve arrows – a place of play and work, of imagination and adventure.

Yet Jack was not loved in the way their mother was loved. At times he could be repulsive. It was with nausea that Sammy remembered undressing him one night. Drunk, he lay flat across the bed while the boy and his grandmother unloosened his clothes. The fat spilled out, pale and slack beneath their fingers, and when they had pulled down his trousers the woman had to close up quickly the fly of the old-fashioned undergarments. The boys often stayed with their grandparents. Then, the pleasures of the evening were curbed by the knowledge that one of them would be expected to sleep in the old people's bed. Once, as Sammy lay tense between the two huge wheezing bodies, his grandfather had wakened and demanded,

"Where do you like to be best? Here or at your mam's? Do you want to come and stay here for ever?"

The boy had been rescued from his confusion by his grandmother.

"Leave him alone,", she said, without turning to them, "How can he answer that? Leave him, you daft man. Go to sleep."

Sammy had wakened as always next morning, cradled tightly against his grandfather's breast.

But normally such memories, for both of them, were hidden things, and now Sammy rose happily from the dirt to help Jack cut a huge bunch of flowers. These were wrapped in newspaper with the lettuce, and Jack pulled a fistful of banknotes from his waistcoat pocket.

"Give her this as well," he said, extracting one, and Sammy set off, carefully holding these gifts to Jack's only daughter.

It was a short walk between the garden and the house. There was a patch of wasteland then an area of builder's rubble. He crossed this quickly and through a narrow lane entered the ring of houses. The street was silent and dust-covered. The houses curved regularly to the left, and though most of them had been occupied for half a year, there was as yet little to mark off one from the rest. A few of the gardens had begun to show some life, and windows held dashes of coloured curtains, but the sunlight lay flat against the pale pebbledashed exteriors, and the shadows were angular and black.

To avoid a pack of dogs that raced frantically into and out of the same gate, he crossed the street and came to a ball that rested in the gutter. He began to play, flicking it against the low brick wall that separated gardens and pavement.

"That's wors," somebody shouted.

He looked around, Ken and Terry Hutchinson stood at their front door. He chipped the ball over the wall towards them and walked on.

Where you going?" It was Terry who spoke, the youngest.

"Just home."

Sammy wanted nothing to do with them. Ken strode around the estate like a man and all the younger children knew, without understanding, the squalid rumours about him. The first time Sammy heard the word shite, it came from Ken's lips. Ken was odious, like the word itself.

"Hey, Ken." Again it was Terry. "Look, flowers."

Sammy pulled the newspaper over the flowers and hurried on. There were feet on the pavement behind him. Peter had told him never

41

to run. He turned and Terry grabbed the parcel and trying to pull it back Sammy split flowers and lettuce across the ground. He moved forward angrily, but Ken came to his brother's side and with his black pointed boots began to grind the flower heads to pulp. With one kick he sent the lettuce bursting onto the roadway, then carelessly pushed Sammy towards home.

"There's plenty left in the garden," his mother said, "Don't let that lot worry you."

But anger and frustration still pricked his eyes as he went upstairs. Peter looked round disinterestedly and asked for his jeans to be passed from behind the door. Sammy threw them over and sat on the windowledge. He flicked through a football magazine, hoping that Peter would start to talk and give him an opening to tell his story, but the older boy lay across his bed, struggling to pull the narrow legs of the jeans across his heels. Sammy asked if he was coming to the garden today. Peter shrugged. He might. He went to the wardrobe, and put on a freshly-ironed yellow shirt, watching himself in the mirror. Sammy wondered. Recently Peter had been inclined to spend a lot of time with the Hutchinsons, and he sensed here an opportunity to regain some of his brother's lost allegiance. Warily, he began to tell what had happened in the street. Peter turned sternly from the mirror. Nobody picked on his brother. Where had he seen them? Sammy answered vaguely, uninterested in the prospect of revenge. If Peter came back with him now, they might meet them on the way, he said. But Peter turned to the mirror again, and said he would come later. They'd find them in the afternoon.

As he left the house, Sammy remembered the five-pound note. His mother sent her thanks with him. She asked if Peter was going.

"He might, after."

She clicked her tongue.

"Never mind. You get back. I don't know what's getting into that lad."

Sammy rarely told his grandfather anything about his life away from him, so it was with surprise that he listened to himself tell, for the third time, the story forced upon him by the loss of the parcel. Jack dismissed its importance, though. He said there was plenty left, and the Hutchinsons had always been a bad lot.

The rest of the morning passed quietly and Sammy forgot the disturbance. They did little work. Sammy fed the hens, scraped their eggs and placed them in cardboard trays in the greenhouse. Jack watered and weeded a patch of leeks, that in the autumn would be entered in competition and set out with their prizes at the club. Mostly, they just sat on the pile of bricks, Sammy playing with one of the new birds, while Jack looked out towards the football games, continually lighting and relighting his pipe. Years before, he had been a professional in the game, and he knew with pride that Sammy shared his love of the game.

It became warmer, and Sammy ran to the shop for lemonade. They shared the bottle, wiping its rim before gratefully lifting it to their lips. Sammy turned away smiling when he saw how the liquid began to draw sweat from the old man's skin. It stood in small droplets above his tightly-fastened collar, ran in thin trickles from below his cap.

Neither of them felt bored. Normally an hour seemed an age to Sammy, but when the distant factory buzzers began to announce twelve-o-clock, he exclaimed at how quickly the first morning of his holidays had passed.

"Aye," said Jack, "It won't be long till you're at that new school of yours."

"No," replied Sammy, feeling apprehensive about that event, which had so rapidly come a little nearer.

They parted at the gate. Jack turned towards the club, where he would spend an hour or two with old friends. Sammy set off for home with a fresh lettuce under his arm and a half crown in his pocket. He had his shirt tied about his waist, and his skin, scuffed with dirt, was tingling after its exposure to the sun.

A scorching afternoon had begun to settle on the estate. Even the children seemed too warm, and they played in the shadows in small sedentary groups. Front doors stood wide open. Old people sat in the shade at the sides of their homes, their battered sun hats a strange contrast to the new buildings. Prams were in many gardens, shades drawn up, their chrome trimmings sparkling. The crying of babies travelled, thin and distant, to Sammy's ears. He smelt warm lunches, heard the small sounds of boiling fat and chinking cutlery. Realising his own hunger, he hurried on, until his own name was added to the sounds in the air.

He looked around, shading his eyes with a forearm. The call came again, and he saw that Peter was sitting with the Hutchisons at the front of their house. As Peter rose and came towards him, Sammy began to feel hurt and betrayed. They were awkward with each other. Peter put his arm around Sammy's shoulders and tugged him quickly and clumsily. The shirt sleeve was brittle and crisp against the warm flesh.

"I saw them about it," said Peter, "They won't do it again."

Sammy said, "Good. Are you coming for dinner?"

Peter held on to him and didn't move. He looked back at his friends.

Ken rose and came to them, grinning, and he, too, drew Sammy towards him.

"Sorry, Sam," he said, "It was nowt really."

Sammy stood stiff and dumb. He rarely spoke in the presence of older boys. He turned away and saw the men arriving home for lunch. In the distance, the road surface was a glistening black pond. Behind him, the voices were lowered in rapid discussion, and then Peter said,

"Hold on, Sammy. Listen. Stay with us a bit. We're going to do something."

He drew Sammy back into the group. Terry ran to join them.

"Are we going, then?" he said.

"Yeah. He's away," said Ken.

They went along the side of the Hutchinson's house and out of the back gate. They scrambled under a row of old hawthorn bushes, where Sammy scratched his skin and had to hold his breath against the stench of excreta. They jumped a wall that had once bordered a line of cottages and came to the waste ground. Here, Ken took from his pocket a brown paper packet which contained what looked like a small rectangular box. He held it teasingly between forefinger and thumb. Sammy tried to echo Ken's grin, but the edges of his mouth twitched and his eyes were sullen. Along with his discomfort, he also felt scorn, that the others could think something so special in this. But he was too timid to leave, and he stumbled through the rubble, clutching his lettuce, close to Peter, wanting to touch him, and wishing they could both go home. They came to the edge of the allotments, and Peter looked down at him.

"We're going to the garden," he said, and looked away quickly.

Terry ran in front of the others, threw the gate open and began to swing on it. Ken pushed Sammy through, but he resisted and looked at Peter.

"Howay, you bastard," said Ken, "Somebody'll see."

Peter stepped between them. He said,

"Come on. It's okay, nobody will know."

Terry was already inside. He had found the box of chicks and was poking his hand into it. Angrily, Sammy told him to leave it. He felt on surer ground with this boy, who was close to his own age.

"Yeah, go on," said Ken, "Stop messing about."

Sammy retrieved the box and put it back into the sunlight next door. He came back and shut the door behind him, putting the room into almost total darkness. Ken went to the only window and pulled aside the square of cloth which covered it. It seemed a familiar movement, and Sammy wondered how often Ken and Terry had been here before. He remained standing as the others crouched in the pool of light and lit their cigarettes. He watched Ken lay his packet on the floor and begin to open it, crackling the paper in the stillness.

They were not cigarettes. Ken lay the box face up in the dust. On its lid was an artless photograph of a woman dressed in thin yellow nylon whose edges were drawn back to reveal unnaturally pink buttocks and legs. Her head was turned and she looked out with a fixed grin at the boys.

"Hell," said Peter, "I thought it was fags."

Ken snorted.

"Like shite. Here, Sammy, get an eyeful."

Sammy moved closer, crouched at a distance from the others while Ken opened the box and lifted out the pack of cards. He knew the shop that showed these cards with magazines in its window. He passed it rapidly, glancing into the window and then into the faces of passers-by, his cheeks hot and damp. At night, in bed, the image of the window often came back to him, and he wished he could stand before it and stare as other boys could.

Ken divided the pile into four and handed them round. Tentative at first, and scared of the others watching him, Sammy began to hold his cards more hungrily. He peeled them over, wanting to find one woman at least who did not, through an arrangement of limbs or clothing, keep her true femaleness from sight. But each picture, in its limited pastel shades, gave only a suggestion of what he wanted to know, and each new set, as the cards were passed around the ring, brought the same lack of illumination.

Terry constantly giggled. Ken leered aggressively. The cards he had first came back to Sammy and now, his pulse calmed, he began to look more slowly. His eyes began to be held by a single girl, her thighs gripped by nylon, her arms laid over her breasts, and he felt the stirrings he had known in bed. What they were, what he might do with them, he had no idea.

They came in waves beneath his skin. They rushed. His whole body seemed to draw itself together and then for the first time it drained away suddenly to a single point. And then he sat back from the circle, drew his knees tightly to his chest, knowing only that he didn't want to look any more and that he wanted to go home. Peter looked up at this movement and put his cards back into the box. He said they would have to leave now, his grandfather would be coming back. Ken scoffed at his fear but Peter shoved him and told him to fuck off. Terry leapt up in temper, but moved impotently out of reach as Peter got up and Ken, blustering, shuffled on his knees to collect the cards.

As he left, Ken let his heel dig into Sammy's side.

"Here," he said, dropping a card onto the floor, "this'll give you something to do in bed."

Sammy sat stock still as Peter cleared up, picking up the cigarette ends, burning them in a small fire with the card, flapping the door a few times to clear the air inside. Then they closed up. Sammy walked stiffly, his limbs queerly weak and angular, Peter's arm draped over his shoulder. Peter made him stop at the edge of the houses and held him tight.

"I didn't know what it would be, Sammy," he said.

As they stood there, Sammy could smell his own body in the heat, and he began to feel a completely new fear of going home.

The house was stifling and steam-filled. Fortunately, their mother was busy and she sent them to hunt out dirty clothes. They gathered a bundle from their room, pulled socks from under the beds. Sammy kept on his shorts, wishing he could burn them.

They sat down to two plates of limp salad. It was tasteless to Sammy. He rushed it, wanting to be somewhere else. He was already finished when his mother came in with some tea. As she went to the kitchen again, she stopped.

"Oh, Sammy, did you get the lettuce?"

Sammy looked down. It was in the greenhouse.

"We'll need it for tea," she went on.

"It's at the garden." His tongue felt thick and clumsy, too big for his mouth.

"Oh, well. You can go up for it later."

He was ill-at-ease, trying to shift from her gaze. She watched him. He held his cutlery tightly, fists resting on the table's edge, trembling.

"Sammy," she said.

Peter rose, as if to distract her attention. She leaned forward and touched Sammy's arm. She said his name again,

"Samuel?"

Her voice rose on the last syllable, mingling inquiry, reproach and concern.

Creeping About

"When the lights go on and the moon comes out," she said, "Be back by then."

He was on the step, gazing towards the fields, imagining her preening herself before the mirror. He heard her scuttling about, heard clothes being pulled across her body, the sharp ejaculations of her breath, her clattering heels on the bare tiles.

"Do me up," she said, and he had to stand and fumble with the zip, pull it up over the wedges of flesh caught tightly by the bra strap. She stood with her arms held high, squeezing lacquer onto her hair.

"Make sure now," she said, "I'll leave you something."

Her. She had gone out, as always, stepping out over his crouched body, her feet clackling down the garden path while her hips swayed from side to side. Then the usual turn, smile and wave from the gate, and the rapid movements away along the pavement. Her.

Now the moon was already up, tangled in the trees at the cornfields edge. He lay down beneath the tips of the ripening corn, where there was still some warmth and he was sheltered from the breeze. Lights had come on in the windows of the housing estate. Soon the streetlights would go on. So what? He would stay here. All afternoon he'd imagined and looked forward to this. Below him, in the common's tussocky square of beaten grass a few boys still kicked a football. He would have nothing to do with them, and they would soon leave. Already the voices of mothers calling their children rose over the rooftops.

Normally, he too would leave now, returning with the others, his hair matted with sweat, his trousers and shoes beaten and torn. He would walk home, hear his farewells hanging in the air, echoing from house walls. Home was often dark and empty. As his sweat cooled, he would press close to the bars of the electric fire. Food was sandwiches and lemonade, the pickings of sweet and biscuit jars. Stockings and under-clothes lay piled on chairs. He wouldn't tidy them.

For months he had become more and more aware of the changes that accompanied dusk. There were always doors opening and closing in the street. He would gaze out of the window, through the funnel of his hands, see fathers pass by, hands in their pockets, straightening their ties, see a gathering stream of men making their way beneath the street

47

lights towards the pubs. But it was movement in the other direction for which he watched. Movement away from the light, towards the edge of the common, where small groups of older boys and girls gathered. He peered towards their shadowy outlines, their flickering matches and cigarettes. They moved constantly across the edge of the darkness, groups forming and breaking, figures joining and detaching themselves at will. Sometimes two would come together, forming a pair separate from the rest. It was all strangely disturbing, and he had only vague intimations of what was going on.

Now the children were leaving the common, kicking the ball and racing in a bunch towards it. Their high voices tailed away into the estate and the common became deserted and still. The patches of gorse opposite took on a brighter yellow, shining like light in the dusk, then fading as night quickened, and the moon began to dominate the sky. He became cold, and heard tickings in the corn around him, the cracking of trees in the cooling air. In the estate doors were slammed and cars were stopping and starting. Then it all stopped. Mothers stopped calling, and it was silent.

He'd told himself for weeks that he would do it, that he would stay here. She wouldn't know, and anyway what did she care? Between them now there seemed to be nothing, after a year of this kind of life.

"Oh," she had said one night, "You're old enough now, eh?" and had begun to go out. Already the closeness of the past was gone. Yes, he was old enough now, old enough to feel different from the other boys and from her. Fuck her.

He stood up, and set off walking tentatively along the edge of the field. He crouched as he came near the houses, and then began to crawl, for though the darkness of the common and the field was normally impenetrable, the moon tonight was unobscured and shadows fell into its pale light.

Already something was happening. He stopped and re-entered the corn. Immediately before him, and between himself and the street, was a belt of hardened mud, littered with dumped furniture and garden waste. Usually he kept away from here, fearing rats, but now he lay close, staring across it. Two boys were at the top of the street, smoking. They muttered together, and only their curses were distinguishable. Beyond them, a group of girls was approaching. Seeing them, he caught his breath. Girls filled his thoughts so often now, girls who darkened their eyes and who were constantly settling their jeans across their hips as they walked the streets.

48

Had she been like these girls? Had she sat on low walls, swinging her legs, sharing whispers, turning to grin knowingly at boys. Had she been like one of the girls approaching now, her body chalked obscenely onto the pavement? Had his father flicked a cigarette butt in a glistening curve towards her feet, before they moved away together into the darkness while others giggled behind them?

"Do you love me?"

The words were whispered, but loudly enough for him to hear. He had watched as they passed his hiding place, waited, then followed them, crawling.

"You know, love me?"

He couldn't see them. Their low voices had drawn him here. He was among the roots of the gorse, his limbs twisted uncomfortably around their stems. In front of him a low wall of rock dropped to a wide ditch covered with soft turf. His heart was pounding. They couldn't be more than six feet away.

"Love you?"

It was the boy who spoke. Their bodies were sliding over the grass. Clearly it was a joke. She was sniggering.

"Oh, if you don't love me..."

The moon was behind him, sending the shadows of gorse and rock into the ditch. If only he could see.

"And I might have a baby."

"Ha!"

She too would be with someone else now. Someone older than the boy in the ditch, with hair on his arms, black hair showing where the shirt collar was opened above a coloured tie. Later he would stand holding her outside a city pub, and whisper loudly at her, get her laughing. Often one came back with her, tiptoeing down the path with her. They'd fill the dark house with their low voices, the loud creaking of furniture, pierce it with his mother's garbled cry.

"I love you."

He said it with a grin in his voice.

"I do."

They had calmed. Hands were caressing clothes. He heard lips opening and closing, irregular breathing. He dared to pull himself closer to the edge, keeping his hair below the tangled gorse, feeling the grass's dampness on his skin. But it was the sound of her breathing, and not the cold, that began his trembling. Clothes were being pulled back. The stiff

49

crackle of denim, and then a long period of stillness and moaning. They moved against each other once more and more clothes were unfastened and pulled. There were grunts of effort, quickening breathing. His head hung over the edge but all he could see was movement and the vague contrast between white flesh and dark clothing.

Often she seemed even to have forgotten his name.
"Up, come on, you, up!" it had been when he'd been found asleep before a flickering television screen.
"Up you go!"
Pulled up and pushed on his way to the stairs, sleepily stumbling past the usual dark figure in the hallway.

Yet during the day came endless bleak gifts, slung at him, or dropped carelessly onto chairs. Toys that resisted his fumbling grip for mere days, sweets that he tipped over garden walls or kicked across pavements. Even whisky, that she offered when she lifted him to her lap, breathing repulsively into his face.
"Do you love me?" she slurred.
His fists clenched on the gorse.
Fuck her.
Fuck her. It came into his head over and over. They said it in the street, littering their savage sentences with the word.
"I'd like to fuck that," they snarled.
He used it only in his head, with only vague understanding. He wanted to see, to really understand. And noises weren't enough. Not the noises from the pair below, or the noises from his mother in the room below. Often he lay in the darkness watching the reflections of headlights glide across the ceiling, trying to analyse the true nature of the events downstairs, but night slipped over, he fell to sleep, or heard the opening and closing of doors, an engine starting, and by morning he was left weary, disturbed and disappointed.

Dew had settled on him, squeezed out of the cold air. He was shivering, and slid back beneath the gorse. He felt small, cold, young. Separated, they tugged at buttons and zips. Something flopped against the wall and fell.
"No babies this time," said the boy.
They laughed, stood up, their long bodies lifting out of the shadow, moving along the slow incline of the ditch, towards the common. He waited, his head turned, watching for their shapes against the light. Soon they passed.

50

He swung over, dropped, sprawled on the turf. Once she had loved him, held him, folded him to her. Tears spilled from his eyes. His hands on the grass felt cold where he had wanted the remnant of their warmth. Hard stones scraped his fingertips. Creeping about brought nothing else.

Hold Me Close, Let Me Go

After years of waiting, I couldn't wait to change, and left still dressed in my mourning clothes. Only as my ship squeezed between the piers and England was absorbed by its mist did I drop them, one by one into the sea. I stood in the bows, looking forward, leaving.

I was thirty. Did I have to wait till then? Is it only when parents are gone that we can leave? Father went when I was twelve. So Mother said. All I remember is how his back was hunched against her spite as he closed the door on us. She said he was drowned soon after, 'lost at sea'. I didn't believe her. For me, lost meant 'might be found again'. He might come through the door again with open arms. He might move our way. Always he had told me on his annual and bitter returns, when he bent close to me, whispering, with his eyes heavy-lidded and turned from her,

"Only one thing to do, daughter, when you've grown. That's to move, keep moving."

I wanted more than that, but always her voice came, inquisitive, laced with fright.

"What you doing? What you saying to the girl?"

"Nothing. Stories. Stories about the sea."

But there were no stories, only a haunting presence, muffled words, furtive efforts to instruct.

"You can go anywhere, do anything, when nothing keeps you here. Look forward to it."

He was scared: this brooding house that claimed him after its year of waiting. Scared of her desire to close him in it. Scared of me, how my limbs clung. I saw it in his eyes – something that might have been love, yes, but also 'Let me go, let me go'. It was our need that drove him out to what she called a death.

"And you might as well know it, girl. He won't come back."

I knew it, but I waited, both for him and for my own time to leave, while she embraced despair as if it were a thing to love.

"And know this, girl. He never loved us. Never. Neither as husband nor father did he love us. You're nothing but his leaving."

That I didn't know. What was this love that had never come to settle with us? Where was it? Soon grown, I went to men and told them,

"Show me love. Fill me up."

I brought them to lie a wall away from her, seeking a love in one room to balance its absence in the next, but they failed me, each one of them, just as their sperms failed on my poisoned diaphragm's taut curve. She applauded me, watching them leave.

"Good girl," she told me, "Never let them back."

There was none I wanted back, none who showed me that love was anything but the moving that left me alone at small pleasurable points of arrival; with pleasure soon followed by recoil to the recognisable place, where she was at the centre, clutching tight as any child. And I mothered her. I tended her. Eighteen years of life I spent on her. Years of waiting, nothing but a remnant of his seagoing. Years of being flung from frantic dreams to frantic dark, with 'Let me go!' my stifled yowl, my whisper. 'Let me go!' with clenched teeth, lips squirming at the wall beside my bed.

She let me go. She abandoned me. She crawled in through my door at dead of night, the emptied bottle raised to me.

"This time I've done it," she told me, her voice more clear then for years, "This time I've gorged myself."

I guided her back into her own room, her own bed, her own absence. I sat stroking her, waiting.

"Didn't I save you from him? Didn't I always keep you close? Help me, my sweet. Don't let me do this. Help me to stop this going on."

I waited. And how it helped to stop this going on.

*

I leaned on the ship's rail, looking forward; the first move, and with all the money from the sold house allowing me to imagine a multiplicity of moves. I travelled south, on the train opened my tiny suitcase like jaws, watched the fine spit of my belongings whipped across the fields. I indulged myself, ate thick garlicked stew, swallowed dark red wine, veering almost noiselessly past Carcassone's red peaked roofs. Pyrenees separated from earth and sky. I sipped cognac, nibbled thin slivers of rocquefort. Always my white-coated waiter bowed. Mais oui, mademoiselle. Tous que vous voulez, mademoiselle. Through an alcoholic haze as I disembarked I saw waiting Le Petit Train Rouge. It lifted me slowly from the coastal plain, around gorges and across slopes where panels huge as villages drained the sun's rays. In the open carriage my skin crept as the air cooled. I was put out at the small silent town edged with its lip of medieval walls; Villefranche de Conflent, whose pedestrian gate I stooped through to find a pretty place, with tiny brooks washing pavements, quiet voices echoing against stone, curtains and home-made quilts hanging out above me, gorgeous against the stone, and stilled air heavy with the scents of coffee, flowers, new bread. I took a room whose balcony hung over flagstones littered with dazzling geraniums. For days I stayed there, walking the long cool corridors inside the walls, winding about me bright new woollen clothes and jewellery of semi-precious stones heavy on my throat and wrists. In the evenings I sat out in the cold street, long tunnel of houselights and children in short frocks playing, emptying myself of England. It was a resting-place, a place to gather breath, a place in which to condition my self to thinner air. Outside the walls, even at night when I lay in my heaped bed, vehicles rolled past on the narrow road, travelling lower, travelling higher.

A taxi took me higher, accelerating past convoys of army vehicles; jeeps and armoured cars trailing hooded guns, lorries from whose drab covers surprised soldiers waved; to Mont Louis, anther stone town high on slopes that fell away in a wide valley from it, protected and threatened by it. It was a larger town, a garrison town. Inside it was the old wall-builder's house, solid as it ever was, surrounded by late tourists with their cameras. I lived by the gates and watched the convoys squeeze hourly through them. At the centre was the wide, fenced-off trampled area where for centuries the garrisons had prepared themselves. I woke to the steady tramping of boots, barked orders and bugles, ate my meals beside soldiers slouched and ill-at-ease, muttering as they watched the skies of autumn thicken above the walls. The winds did not fly over this place, but came into it to whirl trapped through the streets, setting leaves and litter leaping to wild spirals at the junctions. I had a room with deep armchairs, high wooden wardrobes, a fire that was cleaned, laid and lit each morning, but nevertheless I thought of leaving, travelling south again towards the warmer places in which I had always imagined my father. Here I rattled like an unlocked door. I was a dream out of place. All around me the hotel doors were locked. Chambermaids and barmaids went off with their suitcases, waving. I ate inside, alone, the dining room's light lit only for me. "I'll go too," I said, "tomorrow." But the patronne thickened my food, brought it in deep steaming bowls to me. She smiled fondly. On peut rester ici, madame, pendant l'hiver. She grew used to my being there. Tu es bienvenue.

How rapidly, at that height, winter came. Darkness edged out the days. Snow came, blocking the roads outside, lay in the gutters and streets as if filling a trench. The convoys moved out on chains and spikes. White-uniformed infantrymen fanned out across the white meadows on white skis, wearing goggles, with rifles lashed to their backs. All day I heard the cracking of their guns, the booming of their shells. In the evenings they sat nervous and bored at the bars, snapping sudden angers and laughter at incomprehensible jokes. They were disturbed by me and kept turning to me. I thought, It's November. They want the town for themselves. Then I thought, It's me they want for themselves.

I let them come to me, not all of them, not many of them; just the young ones, those far from home, who had a loneliness in their eyes that had not yet become bitterness. I let them roam over me. I watched their wrongly-taught bodies in the firelight, then held them close to me, whispered softly to them. Tout sera bien, tout sera bien. When they went away from me they still wanted me, but I would not let them back.

I did not want Francois, with his English and his talk of England, with his Chartreuse and his beige cigarettes, but he came anyway to sit with me, with the stars on his arms kept the others away from me. I could see his family in his eyes, his wife in the suburbs waiting for him, the children sitting in their desks in rows, each morning chanting praise of the Republic. He was a captain, who told me he had joined up years ago, in order to travel and to act, but he had spent his time being shuffled about the borders of Europe. He hated this wintering, these games. Je veux partir, he said, always to leave; to say, here there is not enough for me, now is the time to go. But I am loue... hired. I am not my own.

Until Christmas I did not know what he expected of me, but then he came angrily, hammering on the glass door that one day locked against soldiers. I was dining with the patronne: lamb with charred sprigs of rosemary falling from it. I stood with him on the doorstep while my food cooled. His eyes were reddened by a long morning's drinking. I am alone, he said, tout seul. Even at Christmas to be locked in here by weather and a uniform. We accepted him in, laid a place for him at our table's edge. He sat there silent and ashamed, hardly glancing at me, until we were left alone, in dusk and candlelight. Through the kitchen's open door I saw the patronne, her eyes advising caution: prenez garde madame.

I took no guard. Outside my room snow thickened on the windowledge. From the streets came drunken parodies of old French carols. We moved towards each other fast and certain as trains on their rails and drew from each other noises that seemed fit to reach England. We woke miles apart, hauled each other back, into the bed where we curled close and warm, and slept again.

I became his, the space around me only for him. The captain's woman, waiting each day in the warm hotel for his return from his games. We expected nothing from each other but the liberating cries with which we filled each other. I told myself it was an interval, packed into the imits of ancient walls and suffocating snow. Once he tried to show me photographs, to spread his memories before me. He asked me, what was my past, my future? But I wanted none of that. Our eyes hollowed as we gazed through candlelight at each other. The only place to go was into that hollowness, out of ourselves. Sometimes I wanted to telephone someone, anyone in England, to say everything was fine, but the idea was an irritation, something to be discarded as I had discarded everything that

stopped me being a simple presence here, a gulf into which I could fall
with him. At dawn I often knew, waking beside him, that I hated him, and
that it was he who kept me empty and thin as always; that I should close
myself to him, take guard, but I abandoned hate, abandoned myself to
this wintering, and despised nothing but the very thought of protection.
And anyway I loved my frail body's strange violations of itself, the way it
made use of abandonment to speed towards destruction; and loved the
way each time I made myself again, my skin re-forming itself after its
dissolution.

In February he claimed leave and helicoptered out over the white
valley below a dazzling sky. Wrapped in bright wool, kicking tracks
through snow, I ran after him. I found myself singing, building snow
mockeries of myself and my captain, Knee-deep, I ran right out yelling at
the miles away inadequate white of the infantrymen. I can see you! Je
peux vous voir!

Next morning I woke nauseated, the child inside me already
sucking me to itself.

He came back furious at his country's lack of need. They play a
game with us, he said – un petit jeux. It is we who allow them to flourish
behind us when they send us out into the cold. They tell us to watch for
them. They pretend to regret our leaving. They forget about us. They
have everything, and imagine we need nothing. Rien.

I held up my hands to him, but in a gesture of protection rather than
welcome. He knocked them away, gripped my hair tight.

"Stop it," I said, "Laisse-moi seule."

He flung my head aside.

"Et toi aussi? You have also played?"

I prepared to leave, sitting with new suitcases by the fire while the
snow diminished on the windowledge, dreaming myself as a winding-
sheet about the child. Already it struggled to break free.

"Maman," it cried, "Laisse-moi seule."

I left my captain by the gate. He shook my hand while his eyes
claimed something ar beyond me.

"I'll leave, too," he said, "I'll leave all this. I'm finished here. I'll go
somewhere they might make use of me, where I can act. Africa, the East.
I'll go so suddenly there'll be no way I can return. Only then might I find
out what I can be."

He kissed my cheek.

"We didn't play. Nous n'avons pas joue."

The taxi crept over the long line of white between its wheels, then
skidded and splashed through slush and running pools. At Villefranche
water poured from the rocks and walls. On Le Petit Train Rouge again I

56

sat in drizzle, covered by plastic, colder now than I had been all winter, but within an hour came to unblemished green meadows, their spring flowers open wide.

*

Banyuls curled close around its beach. Tourists came to sprawl like flotsam among its seaweed and thin slicks of oil. I took a room at the back of town facing stony vineyards and took account there, hoarding loose change, picnicking on cheese and cheap wine. I watched buds break free of their stems, waited for my flesh to swell. I told myself, once you have left somewhere, become foreign in a foreign country, anything is possible. I tried to imagine the next move, to the south, Africa, the Orient, but the child petrified inside me, and I could not move.

I knew she was downstairs, the English woman. I heard her singing, the clattering of her typewriter keys, but I wanted nothing from her, and slipped past her door on silent feet. But she came, with her English greeting, her expensive wine. She said how wonderful it was to share a common tongue. She talked all afternoon; a woman freed by inherited money, who spent her time travelling the Mediterranean shore, migrating with the sun, spinning her anger and her dreams into what she said were incomprehensible stories. She saw how immobile I had become, and told me growth was a journey:

"Only when you leave somewhere can you be born, but you must make use of the leaving, must continue leaving."

She wanted me to imitate her.

"It's easy. You follow your desires, that's all. You're so sweet. Come with me. Imagine a Moroccan summer with me."

Later we lay behind closed shutters on my stripped bed, her hands and tongue searching me, and I welcomed her, the forgetfulness she brought; until she came to rest at my belly.

"A child?" she said, appalled, "You have a child in there? Get rid of it. You can't go any further till you're rid of it."

For days we sat in street cafes, where she stunned me with alcohol and her insistent words. At night, "Let me in," I whispered, imagining that somewhere inside her was the secret of her easy leaving. "Let me in," probing her body as if for some hidden entrance. While she slept I whispered, "I want to be inside you, right inside you. Take me with you. Let me in." She woke filled with spite.

"Get rid of it. What's stopping you? Get rid of it."

I thought it the next move, when she took my hand and led me to George, to his home beneath Perpignan's gutters. George was English, too, and milkwhite and compassionate; failed medical man become writer, assuring me that all would be well. It was nothing, he told me, a small digression in my travelling. He laughed: what traps we found for ourselves, we English, when we went abroad. My child's growth? It had not yet gone too far. Turning away from me, they spoke of words together, how they could catch nothing but their own movement. They caught me staring, silent.

"Nothing's fixed any more," she said, in explanation, "Certainties are gone. Sometimes it seems there's nothing even to be named."

Next morning I let myself be laid out on the white. I let his hands pursue the life in me. I let him arrange me, felt the gentle damage begin to be done. But suddenly I cried,

"Laisse-moi seule!"

It was the child and me together. Its tongue was flapping wildly with my own.

"Laisse-moi seule!"

I snapped tight, curled tight, every exit from myself – eye, anus, vagina, mouth – a tight muscular ring. I leapt and ran from them, and they fell away easily, like fruit rotting from its stone.

*

In Banyuls again, on its brightly-lit beach edged by mountains and sea, I went to lie with the tourists, and every day became browner, tougher, every day felt the child press his nutbrown dome higher. I paddled in streams whose beginnings were melted snow, floated out on their currents as if to be washed to a different seedbed. I practised the disciplines of breathing and muscular contraction and imagined a skill that would thrust the child as far as Africa. On the beach, in the streets, at tables, my belly brought mothers bustling to me, but I smiled only into myself, focusing the sun into my dark centre, and beneath the protection of feigned linguistic incompetence, dreamed myself into being all the places the writer had told me of, with my shores ranged about a sea that was the centre of the world. In the sand I drew maps: barren England, verging on a huge cold emptiness, then this new place, drenched in sun, fruit-filled, curled in perfect closed femaleness around the bright blue pool.

But I couldn't be left alone. I was recognised, and the place closed in on me, wanting me out. As summer swelled, I tried to resist, but the patronne's eyes veered daily to my hidden child. "You will go home soon, madame?" she asked, in her few known words of English. And I nodded, but only at the jerk of my child's complicit laughter, its anticipation of freedom.

We couldn't wait for its arrival here. More and more the patronne wanted to take control. She murmured of hospitals, policemen. We moved. Travelling south was like swimming, heaving through dense water while the child rolled and rolled through its own water, protesting at the hot noise of Spanish trains. Whole families packed in at our side, children and suitcases dropped in through the flapping window. Maize and gross bamboo whipped past in our wake. Northern students, experimenting with freedom, stared into the compartment as into an aquarium, acknowledging the queer amphibians inside. Spain was a coastal strip hidden by its crops, translucent mountains, glimpses of red rooftops and astonished attendants protecting the track's junctions with dusty roads. It lay roaring in the darkness at stupidly long halts in Barcelona, Valencia, Murcia, Granada. I bought my food at the window, from platforms filled with argument and laughter – lemonade in bottles with steel-sprung caps, sandwiches filled with sourly-spiced meat. Three days and three sleepless nights I travelled, ignoring all the efforts made to care for me. Gibraltar, I told them, I have it there. My odour thickened in a pool around me, my weight and tiredness seemed to seal me to the upholstery, until at last I fell into dreams of snow and firelight, icy winds failing against windows.

It woke me, demanding a quick release. The track was ended. I got out, almost waddling, into a place of violent heat, a place in which they despised me. I saw it in their eyes: The English cling to what they have. Go to your own. I walked the hill from the village, saw Gibraltar waiting behind its gates; garrison of apes and English in the narrow gap between ocean and trapped sea. I wanted to stay there with all that in front of me, to wait silently for the strange moments of exit and arrival, welcome and leavetaking, but the child began to strike at me, threatening a pain for which I was unprepared. I walked on, every few moments forced to halt, to squeeze myself, hold it in,. Closer to the gates I began to scream.

"I'm English! Do something! Don't you understand?"

A squaddie peered at me through binoculars. Sunlight disintegrated him. The rock above him fused with sky.

"I'm here! See me! Here I am!"

I fell, and the child, taking its chance, began to muscle out of me with vengeful strength. Then the jeep came. I was lifted across its tailboard, my legs swinging free. Someone yelled gibberish at me, trotted behind with arms outstretched as the jeep moved off, ready to catch anything that might fall out of me. It yanked at me, pulling me off like a discarded skin, ripping me with its haste. The jeep halted at the gates and I was lifted to the ground, English ground, as its head appeared, an outraged dummy's come to make its mischief in public view. The rest slithered out behind, guided by dirty, clumsy fingers. I saw it lifted up, road dirt sticking to its gluey skin. It was purple and bruised, howling its fury.

A boy, premature but all intact. In a glass case, with food and air piped at him he lay motionless, staring, waiting. Everything of mine that had supported him, useless jetsam, had followed him hours later. I was cleaned out, neatly sewn. My belly fell, beginning to search its memory of a former shape. The boys who had delivered him came with flowers, to stand at the bedfoot appalled, fascinated and proud, watching me as if I were something they had been warned of, and feared always to see; but also as if they were homing on me, as if with me their innocence could be both dispelled and turned to strength. I laughed, asking if we had shown them the action they had joined up to see. Pockmarked by too much adolescence, embarrassed by my gaze, they flinched. I directed them to the child, and tried to watch them as he did, strange creatures inhabiting strange spaces outside the glass. Awkward humans, they squinted and twitched, locked out from what they had come to love.

I didn't stand there. I didn't lower myself towards his eyes. I slept and ate, recovering myself, preparing to leave. I was despised for it. This is your child, I was told. It is your purpose to begin loving it. My doctor scorned me. He had Mediterranean skin, a flawless accent. I was verminous to him, a flaunter of English illnesses, searching some dockyard gutter to shelter in. He wanted me back with my child to the place from which I had come. But where was such a place? There were places to which I would go, but how carry him there?

"I'm finished with him," I said, "Nothing needs keep him with me now. I want rid of him."

Next morning, alone, fingering the loose flap of my belly, I shuffled out.

*

"Alone? Toute seule?"

Unprepared for heat, exhaustion, the pain of moving too soon, I had come to sit inside, beneath the rock. I felt his eyes on me as I laid out my food before me, sniggering at the illusion that it might replace all I had lost. He was a sailor, capped and moustached almost in parody of his trade, wearing clothes designed to keep out water, take strain. Unmoved, I stared back at him as he came with his bottle to my table.

"Alone?"

I nodded. Yes, alone. What did he want with me? Love? He would be disappointed. Desires I might once have had were mutilated as my body, were things from the past, memories.

"Tourist? Touriste?"

Again, yes.

He emptied his brandy into my glass, encouraged me to, "Drink. OK? Drink." I drank it, felt it leak through me, heating all the emptied channels inside.

"Tourist. You will go home soon."

He stated, rather than questioned it, and again I nodded; the easy answer, meaningless. He was middle-aged, middle-eastern. He regarded me as if he were waiting, but for what? I returned to my food, imagining his scorn: the English, the cold English.

"To England. Home to England."

"Yes, home to England."

I didn't look up. Irritated by him, I wanted him gone. It was no time for welcoming a man.

"OK." the flat tone of disappointment. I glanced at him. He had recoiled, to dejected lips, hurt eyes. "OK, miss. Never mind."

"Drink." He had come to share his absence, nothing more. I poured him wine. "Drink this." I wanted to tell him: don't go, stay here, share what you can. "Drink. OK?"

He drank, with lowered, heavy-lidded eyes.

"And you?" I said, "Where will you go?"

He shrugged: anywhere. But it was his opening.

"Look, miss. Home, my home. Yes, look."

I took it, a tiny sun-faded print, its edges curled and torn; small whitewalled house brilliant in sun, with silhouettes of children and wife arranged against it, only their smiling distinguishable on their dark. He pointed, naming each one, and spread his arms to show how much they'd grown.

"Family. Home. Far away."

A simple statement of his condition, but in his eyes a depth of loss in which, with too much drinking, he might drown.

"And how far must you go before you go back again?"

Once more he spread his arms, a world's width of travelling. Too far. I knew it, and knew that for him there was nothing else to do. We drank again. I told him,

"My father. He went to sea."

"Ah."

"His coming home always made up for his leaving."

He waited. For what? Forgiveness?

"He loved me. I always knew he loved me. At home or at sea he loved me. The children always know."

He leaned and touched my hand. I held him tight on the surface of his loss. In touching me he believed he touched everything from which he was separated, and for a moment we shared that sad uninhibited affection known only to those who do meet in small cafes a thousand miles and years from home, to drink, and share their absence. And I wanted to release it, after its two decades of being stifled inside me, to say: I love you, I love you.

"Take me with you. Just for today."

We took each other to a small room above the cafe, where I could conceal nothing. I had to tell him of my child, my emptiness, but he was familiar with a body stunned by birth, and he tended me, wrapping himself around me. The words he whispered were words of encouragement, not scorn.

"Who am I to speak? Look at me. I am no father. You did right to have your child. Whatever you do afterwards, you were right."

With silent lips we calmed each other. We waited.

"Love me. Please love me."

We poured into each other, each everything the other missed. Outside, in fading light, ships moved slowly between sea and ocean, ocean and sea. Inside, love was given freely, without any desire to restrain.

Next morning, I stood with him at our door, wished him well and from the window watched him walk quickly away, going back to sea.

*

I came into view. He hadn't moved. Still unnamed, he lay still staring from his glass. I leaned towards him, calling myself Mother.

"He won't be ready for a while, but you can stay with him. Once we're certain you can care for him, you can take him home."

What was he watching, this doctor at my back? Quickly-solved clinical depression, relentless mothering? And what did the child watch? Was I anything? Was there anything to link me with his long-locked travelling? After his *let me go* did he now call Keep me close? There was no way of knowing. He was silent, a waiting thing.

"In the meantime, arrange your journey. For his sake, I recommend flying."

More days, waiting for my child to leave, with him day and night in the foreign room asking him to hurry, hurry. He came out almost unleashed, a second birth, in which he fought at my breast for anything I could give, and made me retreat to *let me go*; how much must I spend on you? But touch, and the grip we had to share, began an inward journeying that in spite of all confusion on the surface carried us down to each other's centre, where we were found whispering with joined tongues; a half-

62

heard muttering at first, but within a few days sharped to:

"Hold me close but not too close; let me go but not too far."

Sailing out, and then North, in the slow recoil after one year away, it was autumn we approached; and England behind steel sea, beneath steel sky. I looked forward to it. In the bows I carried my child, foreign seed, telling him, There. You see it? There. We'll winter there.

And we would winter there, but only until we were ready to move again, hand in hand this time, across the sea and the indifferent earth, far out towards the place where he would speak out calmly from the day's calm light,

"I'm ready, mother. Let me go."

Minimal Damage

She's gone at last, after all her hints, that were intended, I suppose, to draw me away from my work, to make me reclaim her. I came out from my room to find her sleeping. Her legs gripped me as I crawled in beside her. She pulled me close, sucked at my cheeks with lips. Her eyes gleamed with reflected light, pleading. I turned to her, but she was all dried out, with nothing but sediment between her legs. Until I was almost sleeping she reassured me: "I still want you, I still want you." Then silently drew herself down my body to take me in her mouth.

Next morning she sat high above the pillows. I was hardly awake.

"I can't stand you not wanting me," she said. Watching me, waiting for my reply. "I kept hoping, that if your writing worked again... but you don't even want that now."

I said nothing. She had to go on.

"And I think that if I could just go away somewhere, on my own, only for a while...."

I stared at her. Her mouth kept opening, but had stopped saying words.

"Where are you going?" I asked.

Already she's gone. Already I imagine her entombed in Cliffal, embalming herself, surrounded by fine foods and furnishings to decorate her afterlife...

The girl went to Cliffal, and found that memory was all wrong. She had seen it from the sea, years ago, when she was still young, unmarried; from her father's boat, when she stood up as they rounded a headland, calling for them to, "Look, look, can't we go there rather than going on?" But they only smiled and she could only watch as the tiny white houses above the harbour turned golden as the sun sank behind them, as gulls poured from the sky at returning fishing boats, as the breeze pushed them on towards lights that were being switched on further to the south.

When the boy said, "Where are you going?" that image swam up through her.

They must have been miles out. He drove her to a town squeezed into a narrow fault in the cliffs. Paint peeled from its walls, gutters and fences were cracked, everywhere people shuffled in plastic, huddled in doorways. The harbour was flat black mud, a litter of stranded starfish, tyres, frayed ropes tethering dinghies that leaned awkwardly across each other. It stank of petrol, old fish. Old women, singing, picked things from the angles of stones and mud. Beyond them was an empty monotonous grey sea.

He left her outside the hotel, that was jammed in between the harbour and the cliffs, and went off waving.

Inside she found warped linoleum floors, twisted furnishings, stained portraits of sailors, paintings of rescues in storms. The owner, with his purple lips and fluttering jowels, wheezed,

"We weren't built for guests, see, but the way things are now…I sleep in the afternoons, see…"

But at the limit of the dark cramped stairway he opened her door to such a difference. There were plants everywhere, with large oiled leaves. Ornamental oil lamps glowed. The wood was polished and dark against patterned rugs, floral walls. On the high soft bed white sheets were folded across a dazzling yellow counterpane. And he had left her wine, tiny pottery dishes of pastries, olives, wrapped sweets.

"We got it ready for you, see…"

She sat late, drying herself, cleaning the salt from her skin, spreading creams on it. The only light came through the small square window, beyond which, at arm's length, was the blackness of the cliff. She watched it fade. From downstairs came the murmur of few customers, and later there was the diminishing noise of their heels on the cobbled streets. She thought of the boy, of how joyless he had become, of how pleased he would be now.

This morning she wakes to the dull slapping of the sea. Water trickles on the cliff. Closing her eyes again, feeling the counterpane on her chin, the warmth of her flesh, its smell, she could sleep for years…

And I am left here, in my own small room, with the sparse instruments of my craft – desk, chair, paper, pens. The city below me is obscured. Only the sky is visible. From outside, none of her clattering, none of her entering, wheedling like a child. No "Any chance of seeing you today, sir?" None of her scorn, her "Can't you see you're no good, that it's all gone, that all you ever had was one lucky stroke that's perverted your whole life."

A lucky stroke: my book, composed in the dazed year before my marriage. That was the perversion, a narrative when I believed a narrative existed, and thought that words like love could be used as simply as words like food and room.

Till now, everything has been waste, a burden. Now at last I lean over the desk, beginning.

II

Once there were two houses, that looked to each other across long back gardens divided by a high privet hedge. In each of the houses lived a child, a girl in one, a boy in the other. Their rooms faced each other's, and they became accustomed, at night, to seeing the other's light switched on and switched off. Occasionally, they would see each other, a pale shape in the darkness when the light was extinguished and the curtains opened. The boy, wanting to see more, began to stare. He would rest his head against the sill in his own darkness, and wait. In this way, he became familiar with the shape and movements of the girl. Soon, the girl's attitude began to reflect his own. When her light was extinguished and her curtains opened, the paleness of her face became perceptible above her sill. Each of them knew that as they watched, they themselves were watched. Sleep, when it came, was filled with the other's image.

The girl began the changes when one night, late, her light was switched on again, and the boy saw her standing at the centre of her room, showing herself in her white nightgown. He copied her, and for many nights they faced each other, smiling, dressed in their nightclothes, often waving. Soon they stood naked in the light.

Each of the houses had a door which led into its long back garden. The boy knew, when he stepped out of this door for the first time in the dead of night, and stood waving from the darkness below his window, that she would come out from her door into her long back garden, and would come to meet him below the privet hedge.

Below that hedge, during dozens of sleepless nights, they learned from each other the peculiar habits and activities of adults.

Years later, he told the girl that she had learned nothing in growing, that she had remained fixed in childhood. She said,

"It was you. You dazed me. I missed all that sleep for you, spent the days thinking of you. All this time it's as if I'm only half-wakened."

A postcard has come. A view of Cliffal from the sea.

"All changing for the better – sun, blue sea and sky..."

Also a photograph of her, sitting on the harbour wall, laughing, her forearm raised against the sun, her skirt tucked childishly into her underclothes. It has been taken by her friend, the landlord. She tells me how friendly he is,

"He says they need people to come here, to reinvigorate the place, to make it like it was. Once it *was* as we remembered it. I keep imagining us, living in one of the houses by the harbour, and it seems not an impossible dream. Love, Angela. P.S. If you came to visit me, to see...(?)"

Her face beams from the photograph. I throw it to the floor, then lift it, pin it beneath one of her gifts, a paperweight, blossoms suspended in a crystal dome.

"This is from me," she had said, giving it, "An effigy of something living."

She is in her tomb. She consorts with the dead. They tickle each other with illusions of life before the grave.

Her messages coincide with messages from myself, from habits that go unsatisfied. Most habits are easy, easy to satisfy or to ignore. Regardless of us, the heart goes on pumping, air squeezes, fluids squash beneath the skin. We service the demand for sustenance, for somewhere to splash waste. But the habits of desire press us hard. If we find no place to empty ourselves of them they'll crush us, humiliate us. Years ago I remember staring through the cracked frames of locked doors at other boys who tried desperately, their faces clenched, to empty themselves across torn and trodden photographs of something vaguely reminiscent of a woman, and from my high flat I often look down through the night towards that peculiar part of the city riddled with tiny streets where shops are stacked with ludicrous magazines, doors open to rows of desolate booths where films flicker, start and stop and endlessly rewind, where tiny cellars are filled with the odour of shifting frustrated bodies; where customers wander, horribly submissive to their wants, sperm dribbling to their thighs.

I have never known such helplessness, but I begin to dream, and wake to no remedy. Thoughts of women creep over me, make my body fidgety, my mind ill-at-ease. I cannot work.

Last night I left the flat, made my first unfortunate attempt to discover calm. I found a girl by a railway station willing to come with me. Called Susan, perhaps in her late teens, she talked with the easy intimacy of the young, of her dream to be tied to no person, no place.

"I'm a traveller, emotionally, physically. I give nothing."

I pretended to listen, thought myself free from the need to talk, to follow the drab social procedures that accompany sex, but she stopped and turned to me.

"You think that's awful, don't you?" she said.

"What is?" I asked, confused.

"Giving nothing, caring nothing."

I said that I thought nothing of it. "But for me," I said, "well, one can't both work and be a traveller."

She asked what work I meant, laughed when I told her.

When we arrived in the street below my flat and looked up at the high building she laughed again.

"You won't need to leave before morning," I said.

She stepped back from me, and held out her open palm. In it was the black stock of a knife. She pressed a catch and the blade snapped out.

"You're all rapists, aren't you?" she said, "Get back to your work, mister."

She turned back towards the city centre, refolding the knife by pressing it against her hip, still laughing.

It's she I've been dreaming of, her young skin. Habit, asserting itself.

I need a release, but I need it to be as efficient an act as feeding. I need practical uninvolving women, straightforward as shopkeepers, functionaries to loosen my mind.

When they became adults, they were able to be more open about their needs. Their garden games finished. They began to acknowledge each other in streets. They began to call at each other's door, and took each other away from their parents, from his mother, who was alone, and from her father, who was alone, to afternoons among sand dunes or in the backs of cars. They began to talk, for though the boy had until then disliked the feeling of words in his mouth, he knew that this was the only way to ensure that she would stay with him. In each other's house, their partnership was praised. The boy's mother, smiling at the girl, said.

"It's what he needed. You bring him out. I'd never have believed that someone so young could do it."

The girl's father questioned the boy. He asked about ambition, about how he would direct his life. The boy sat with him, said that he had dreams, but knew the need for secure foundations. He was studying then, building for a future. The girl intervened.

"But that's not the important part, is it?" she said, "He's going to write, aren't you?"

Everyone smiled.

In the summer the four of them travelled together. They sailed in her father's boat, and challenged each other to name the towns and villages above the shoreline.

That autumn, the boy stopped studying. He began to write his book, telling no one, working far into every night, hours past the time when he had waved the girl to sleep. During the day, they noticed with concern his tiredness, said he mustn't work so hard. The words leapt from him to the page.

By spring it was finished, and he sent it out into the world he wished to enter. His publisher wrote in amazement 'that someone so young should write with such maturity.' The boy went to the others now. "But why did you not tell us?" they asked, and he smiled, said it was because they would have told him to stop. He was filled with joy at this sharing of success after the long solitude of writing. They leaned close, in celebration. They said it wa a triumph of youth, of an innocent talent nourished by warm relationships. He looked at the girl and said,

"Without you, I could never have done it."

It was the story of how confusion, anger and inarticulacy can be overcome by a woman's love. He had come to believe such things, and had called his book Becoming Real.

The wedding was the consummation of the celebrations.

The boy and the girl agreed that maturity involved cutting the ties of childhood.

They came to the city, and lived in a small apartment high above the streets. One of its rooms became a study for the boy, from which he was going to repeat his success. The girl busied herself with furnishing the home, with caring for his needs. During the day, while he worked, she wrote long loving letters to the parents, giving them the news. There was little news.

The women I look for are easy to find. They stand in a deceit of window-shopping, or of awaiting a known friend, but are quickly alert at approaching slow footsteps. With them, desires and promises are things simply for transaction. Though I feel an intruder in their rooms, and feel hurried into departure, I keep remembering Angela, of how her enticements had become utterly unsatisfactory for both of us. They fake everything, of course, but it's their work, and how are they to know I don't need to share in their illusions? It's the easy cold contentment they bring that frees me. I work on. Cards and letters pile up, unread, beneath the paperweight. Like the final letter she wrote to her father, not realising he had died.

Sometimes the parents came to visit. The girl explained the boy's reluctance to join them in her room, or to accompany them in trips into the city, by saying that his work demanded his full attention.

"People don't understand what it involves," she said, "It needs a total committment, of energy and time."

But she could not explain his sullenness when he came out from his room in the evenings. He was cold. He stared at them, found them a burden. They sat low, in deep chairs, not looking at each other, embarrassed when they spoke. The parents began to stay for shorter periods, to visit less often. Perhaps they said,

"They don't want us there. They have their own life now. It's understandable, I suppose."

Or perhaps they saw how he had withdrawn from his wife also, refusing to pretend to an emotion he no longer felt. When they were alone together even the sight of her was a hindrance to him. Words, sentences, poured constantly through his mind, but so often she was there, disrupting them, refusing to accept the long cold silences.

"You care nothing for me, nothing," she said, "I know where your mind is, all the time, and it's not with me."

There were always answers in him, leaping out at her.

"And you! All you want is to fasten yourself to me, get me to make up for your own failings. It's envy you have for me, not love. You can't love."

She shrank away. She became more silent, demanded him less often. He thought, she's separating from me. She cannot bear solitude. She'll soon be leaving.

When her father died, they went back to the old town. The girl knelt by her father, weeping, clasping her hands. The boy stared at her helplessness. The body was

69

wax, a piece of false fruit, nothing. He went to his mother's house, looked out across the long back garden. His mother said,

"Come back to make a home there. Live there."

He looked at how old she had become, and contemplated never having lived in this place. She talked about their first years there, when he was a child.

"You hardly went into the garden," she said, "and it was for you I wanted it."

He paid her no attention. He was thinking of how difficult it had become to use words, which had once come so freely. Of the letters he received now:

"...you have abandoned the narrative macrostructure, put nothing in its place... your experiments are excessively laconic.. disconnected images... statements of bleakness... The necessary revelations do not take place..."

Within months, his mother was dead. The boy found that each death brought a lightening of his burden. As to another death, he looked forward to the girl's departure.

She remained for years.

This morning, a strange thing. Susan came back. I heard a knocking at the door, the first such knocking for weeks. I dreaded the reappearance of Angela. She stood there grinning. She said.

"I keep remembering you. You got the knife treatment, right? It meant nothing. Are you letting me in?"

She was easy, relaxed, smiling when she said she felt awful about it. I said it was nothing. I had forgotten about it.

She is sleeping in my bed now. I am in my room. She has taken a job in a club, working as a striptease artiste. She said it laughing,

"That's the word, isn't it – artiste?"

She lives in a hotel behind a railway station. She works all night, sleeps all day. She says she's sure her bed is slept in by someone else at night. She's been asked not to return there until after eight each morning, and to leave before six. Each day she sleeps on clean crisp sheets.

"They know I know, and I know they know I know, but nobody mentions it."

She says she enjoys her life, living easily off the greed of men. Her skin is just as I dreamed it. I asked her to show me her act, but she said no, that was for her slavering audience. She will, though, I'm sure.

The girl said she could not grow, that she was only half-wakened, and she blamed her husband. The boy knew it was true, and knew that he could not grow because of his wife. He thought, my whole life has been a falsehood. I was led to say the wrong thing, to write the wrong things, because of her. He scorned her, and though at the beginning his scorn had often been pretended scorn, and his anger pretended anger, more and more they began to be real. He said,

70

"There's something inside me that cannot get out because of you, and which you would kill."

She said,

"You have already killed me."

On his own, sitting in his room, he knew that blame was meaningless. He knew that it could be said that their waste was simply the product of windows and long back gardens, but he knew that wherever the blame lay, the waste would only be finished when she went away.

One morning as he was waking, pressed close to her familiar flesh, he heard her voice,

"I can't stand you not wanting me any more... I kept hoping, that if your writing worked again... but you don't even want that now... and I think that if I could just go away somewhere on my own, for a while..."

He thought, at last. He said,

"Where are you going?"

III

Susan has been wonderful. All is fluent since she came.

I came out from my room that day to find her already awake, sitting half-clothed on the bed. I wanted her again, but she pushed me away, grinning, saying she would soon have to go. While we ate, she talked of herself, as usual. Her work at the club was to be temporary. She had contacts in many agencies, there was much interest shown in her. She was to model clothes, to adorn commercials, to wriggle before cameras and become rich. She found it all hilarious.

"You show them a face and a body of a certain form, and immediately they begin to drool."

She was fascinated by the flat, the contrast between my study and the other rooms. She laughed at the dust that lay thickly everywhere in the living room.

"You can tell a lot about a person by looking at the rooms he lives in," she said.

"This room's nothing," I said, "Mine is the bare one, with instruments for work."

"Ha. I feel the presence of an absent woman."

It made me laugh.

"A nice way of putting it," I said, "She left ages ago."

As she went out to work, I asked if she might come back next morning.

"I might just do that," she said, stepping out with a playful, but nevertheless seductive, rolling of her hips.

That night I kept watching the clock, wondering how late her club stayed open, imagining her skin against mine. Daylight came, streamed in at the window, the city began to roar. She did not come, and all day I kept peering down into the streets.

It was several days before she did return,

"Well, I did only say I *might* come," she said, "The other mornings I thought, no, why bother? But today I thought, why not?"

She stepped past me, led me by the hand to my bed. She made no pretence of having come to satisfy another other than sexual need. When we were finished, she said,

"Are you going to work now? I'm tired."

It was she who suggested the arrangement that has worked so well for both of us. Just as the light was fading she came into my room. She asked how my work was, and I said it was fine, she must be good for me.

"I found these," she said, spilling Angela's letters and cards across the desk, "Curiosity is one of my minor vices. Do you mind?"

"They're nothing to do with me now," I answered.

I glanced at one of the pages. It spoke of spring becoming summer, of freshening breezes in Angela's life. It asked me to visit, to see.

"She loves you."

"I know. It became a habit with her."

"And how pretty she is."

"Pretty? I suppose so. But also dried out and stale." I pressed my head against her breasts. "Not desirable, not tantalising." She giggled at the flattery, held me close, said,

"A man like you, any man, how do you manage now she's gone?"

I drew back from her and told her of how I found women in the streets.

"That's how I found you, remember?"

She roared with laughter, and I tried to pull her to the floor, to take her, there in my room.

"Not now," she said, grinning at my discomfort, "I've got a proposition to make. You're much like me. You have a few simple needs. If I stayed here we could satisfy those needs in the most comfortable way possible. You get what you want, without having to go out for it. You continue working, with the least disturbance. I get a bed, a place to rest and sleep. What could be better?"

Now it was I who grinned. She stepped back towards me, loosening her clothes.

It is ideal. There is a woman here I find beautiful and desirable. Though she lives here, we meet only for short periods at each end of the day. I do not sleep with her. Even during the nights when she does not

72

work she does not trouble me, but spends them in the living room, poring through magazines, comparing the photographs in them with the many photographs she has of herself. When we meet, she talks profusely, but it is rare that I am required to be attentive. My answers and comments are nothing but her punctuation. She has freed me.

She shows little interest in my work. She cares nothing for it. Once she asked how I was able to live without paid work, and how Angela was able to live away from me, in leisure. I told her of the sale of parents' houses, and I told her about my book, how it was on the shelves of any bookshop she cared to enter.

"A bookshop?" She laughed. "I never read."

I laughed with her, and told her of the people who had written to me saying that my book had changed their whole lives.

"A book do that? You must have idiot readers."

"It's true. They lap it up, and it's all lies."

"But that what books are – lies, making things up, pretending."

"Usually. But not always. Now I show people how they really are, not how they would like to be."

"There'll not be many wanting to read that, then."

I shrugged. That meant nothing. I find I don't even want readers now. I just write, and send nothing beyond my room, and though the book is a catalogue of illusions, it feeds me, allows me to pursue truth. I said,

"You're right. They don't want to be confused, or to be shown their emptiness. But I won't feed their delusions, or give them escape. I accept they don't want to read me yet. I don't really care."

Why did I talk about my work? She neither understood nor was she interested, and anyway, talking is always a failure. Only the written word can contain any meaning. I stopped talking, and was relieved when she began preening herself in front of a mirror. She must have continued thinking, though, for as she was leaving that night she said,

"You're wrong. You can't show people as they really are, but I can. They watch me and slaver."

One morning I expect her to take it into her head not to return to me, and it won't matter, because the whole simple, superficial arrangement has no meaning for either of us. As she said, we are alike, sharing a spite for those who cling to others, wanting them to compensate for what is lacking in themselves. We need no illusions of closeness. I've told her. I said,

"One morning you'll be gone, and I'll hear nothing from you again. And it won't matter, that's what's so good about it all."

She smiled and said, "Yes, we're safe from loving each other."

"You'll leave as easily as you came, leaving no burdens."

She shrugged. "What else?"

When I think of Angela, the continual pressure of her needing me, thinking me heartless and callous, pestering me with questions, unspoken demands. How different it is with Susan – not caring, not caring at all...

IV

As she leaves here, and as she returns, she is followed. She hears their heels on the pavements, their breathing in the shadows. It is their silence that is unbearable.

"If they would only speak to me," she says, "or approach me. I could show them how scared they are, and send them running. But that silence... It's me that's scared."

And letters have begun to arrive for her here. They come from men who have heard recommendations, who have seen her working. They can come at any time, with cameras, help her career. Lechery lies just below the surface of their careful phrasing.

"Is this what they meant," she says, "by giving me circulation?"

She says her agencies have failed her. She talks of promises not kept: being photographed in the tropics, below palm trees, in surf, her face being used in billboards, newspapers, magazines.

"And they send creeps with instamatics to dribble on me."

She has been with me less than a month and already she talks this way. She expects too much too soon. I talk of patience. I say, look at me, how I accept that it may be years until I bear fruit.

"I don't have years," she says, "In years I'll be as old as you."

Last night she wasn't working. I got up. She was slumped in a chair, dozing, magazines piled at her feet. From my own drowsiness, I felt a spurt of desire. Why didn't she come to bed? I asked. She shook her head, said she was thinking.

"Do your act for me," I said, "You'd be doing it anyway, now. It can't take long."

Her lips curled. She said,

"You would grunt, try to control your breathing. I would hear your wet swallowing and feel your eyes on me. I would hate you and I don't want to feel anything for you. I don't want to see you. Go to bed."

She'll be leaving soon, and I don't want her to, not yet. I'm using her, writing of a woman like her, and a man who watches her each night. She is his only illumination. His days are spent in anticipation of her movements. His flesh creeps, fluids are squeezed out. For her, he is a regular pathetic shadowy face at the edge of her stage. She thinks, I give him the bleak reality of his little world.

I need her here longer, to explore the strange contrast between her careless superficiality, and her conviction that she can strip away the surface of a world.

This morning, as she slid into bed beside me, she said,

"If ever I do show you, I must be able to see you as clearly as you see me."

V

The days in hospital are vague, shadowy. For the first time in my life everything inside me formless, breaking up into noise, not words. After the first burning pain, a total lack of it, of any feeling. I remember my mother swimming into view, a suggestion that I go to her. I must have turned away. She had soon gone.

I came out of it to their questions. Who did this? Who could do this? My wife was in constant touch, they said. Did I want her here? I pretended confusion. I shook my head. I said, no, she's dead.

They spoke of a future. They said, in such a case the damage to the organism is minimal. But the effects are immeasureable. They said, working together we can rebuild your life, all is not lost.

I came back to the flat. They pester me still, but I resist. Soon they will be gone, all of them. I begin to gather myself, for the cold solitary life I always wanted...

The girl who now came to stay with the boy was the same age as his wife when he had married her. She had the kind of body that dreams are made of. Without loving any part of her, he desired her fiercely. She was a beautiful undemanding functionary for his wants. She said she made men real, but she found the process of making men real sickening, and she wanted to be distanced from it, to travel, to leave only images of herself for men to look at. He wanted, just once, to watch her, in order that he might explain her better, that he might describe her.

One evening he was standing at the window of his tiny room, staring into the dusk. Below him the streets were already glistening. He was composing this girl in his mind, considering the relationship between her smooth skin and the glossy covers of magazines; how her dancing in dark clubs echoed her dancing in the dark spaces of men's minds, how she travelled over surfaces, avoiding the nets of relationships, emotions, thoughts; how her urgency was the urgency of youth, her perfect body threatened by the effects of time; slackness, networks of tiny lines would come to ravage her. He could hear her shuffling about inside. He heard her come to his door, enter his room, *come to stand by him. She asked about his work. He said it was coming. He thought, she's stopped grinning, already she's carrying failure, soon she'll be leaving. She said,*

"I'm thinking of going away, trying somewhere else. I'm getting nowhere, here."

"And will it be better, this somewhere else?"

"Who knows? But I can't be like you, sitting still, waiting."

"Where will you go?"

"I don't know. I don't think it matters."

He put his arm around her. He had expected this, but since she had come, it had been easy to make words do as he wished. He would have to go out again, searching. Habits would become an encumbrance once more. She took his hand.

"I thought I might do an act for you," she said, drawing him out of the room, "Then we'll be finished."

She took him to the bed, told him to sit naked on its covers.

"You might want me afterwards," she said.

Sitting there, he felt unprotected, as if he also were a performer. He tried to smile.

"Shall I imagine music?" he asked.

"Anything," she answered.

She sat back in an armchair, her robe loosely fastened so that it fell open across her tights. She was still at first, with her eyes closed, until as if waking she began to twist in her chair, lifting her arms and opening her thighs, allowing the robe to slip. Her eyes opened, but she looked down at herself, and he could watch without being watched. He sat forward, in anticipation. She loosened the cord at her waist, began to touch herself delicately with her fingers. He coughed, tried to control his quickening breathing. She lifted her thigh to the arm of the chair, leaned over to pick a mirror from the floor. With it she watched as she opened herself to him. He saw her moisture gleaming, heard it slipping. He wanted to go there, bury himself there, but he kept back, wanting to follow to the end, wanting to stare deeper into that red wordless mouth.

The end came quickly. Her hand dropped to her thigh, the mirror to the floor. She became motionless again, exposed to him. All that was left was his breathing, the tightness of his eyes, the throbbing of desire and blood.

"Is that it?" he said. His voice was trembling.

"It's enough. You can come now, if you like."

She looked at him for the first time as he scrambled from the bed towards her.

"It's what I imagined," she said, "Sitting in the darkness, pop-eyed, grunting, terrified." She pulled her legs wider. "Come on. Come deep. Isn't it what you want?"

He scrambled across her, buried himself between the folds of her wonderful skin.

The first wound was made beneath his shoulder blade. Air screeched from him as he was pushed to the floor. He saw the black stock of the knife between her fingers, the blade running with his blood, her hollow careless eyes. He lay hours, dreaming his death, woke to blood flowing and congealing, to desperate high noises in his head. He struggled on all fours, his mouth groaning for help, slewed over stairs and landings, came to a doorway where he dragged himself erect. Others stepped out of the darkness, stepped back, made around him a ring of frightened faces. He tried to reach them, held out to them the small piece of himself that had been cut away.

In hospital he emerged from the dark spaces in himself, to white sheets, white walls, sunlight streaming across him. To their demands that he explain. He stared back at them. They wanted a story, a way to understand. He said nothing. He told himself, I am gone from their world, to a place where words explain nothing. I have no connections here. Let them be confused.

He came back to his high empty flat and thought, they've gone, all of them. Dead. Death clears the world for those left living. Even desire, its instrument gone, is gone. I begin...

I cannot go on.

VI

They say words used properly can precipitate change. They want me to talk to them, to say how I feel. I cannot.

So they say, you're a writer. Write the words we need. You must come out of yourself, and into the world again. All is not lost. Somewhere out there is a woman loving and kind enough to ignore your disabilities.

Somewhere out there...

I went to Cliffal, found it imagined all wrong. I sat on the harbour walls, waiting. The water rose before me, lifting dinghies that separated and began to bounce on tiny waves. From the horizon other boats approached, surrounded by birds. People hurried past me, came out from their houses to gather at the harbour, calling to each other, pointing.

I kept turning to her hotel, to its single long window above the door where her clothes hung drying. Behind billowing curtains I could see her. She came to the window and waved, and others on the harbour waved to her. She came out laughing, rushed past me, calling out that she wasn't late. She didn't turn. I might have been dead.

The boats came in and jostled each other, landing. Boxes of fish were thrown up, exchanged for rolled bundles of money. I watched Angela's hands among it all, heard her hilarity as she held long fish by their tails.

I returned to my car, sat with its panes closed tight. They followed me, a knot of people not seeing me, touching each other, their eyes turning from face to face. They sat on benches in the shade against the hotel wall. Angela balanced drinks on a tray. A man at her shoulder carried food. They sat with each other, smiling, heads dipping to each other as they talked, wiping their chins, pointing to the sea. On the harbour women were singing, pulling their men up to the walls.

I wanted to be silent, dead, but at the noise of the car Angela, right round in her chair, turned to see me. She saw me, and wanted me gone. She writes,

"Andrew, I saw you, and seeing you there, in Cliffal, made everything plain. You were a stranger. I have come not to want you. That day you were here, we had the first landing of fish in Cliffal for a decade. The harbour has been cleared, the whole town cleaned. I am part of these changes. Can you understand that only now am I becoming real? But why do I write such things, when to you they are only illusion? For you, the world is a single mind in a single room. I could never get in. Perhaps when you came here you thought you wanted me. Did you see that you did not? Go on with your work, Andrew. That's where your reality is."

I drove back through the night, below aeroplane lights that dived into the outskirts of the city, past posters of Susan's face superimposed on the tropics, smiling, welcoming me home. To my high small flat and its instruments.

I told to use them, and I cannot. I am told to speak, and I cannot. I am told to enter the world. By day, I piece together fragments of Angela's mysterious and disconnected story. At night, I go down into the city, wander the peculiar streets of my desire.